Jimmy Gownley's
AMELIA RULES!™

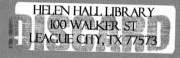

What Makes You Happy

Atheneum Books for Young Readers
New York London Toronto Sydney

Spotlight

VISIT US AT
www.abdopublishing.com

Reinforced library bound edition published in 2011 by Spotlight, a division of the ABDO Group, 8000 West 78th Street, Edina, Minnesota 55439. Spotlight produces high-quality reinforced library bound editions for schools and libraries. Published by agreement with Atheneum Books for Young Readers, an imprint of Simon & Schuster Children's Publishing Division.

Antheneum Books for Young Readers
An imprint of Simon & Schuster Children's Publishing Division
1230 Avenue of the Americans, New York, NY 10020

Printed in the United States of America, Melrose Park, Illinois.
052010
092010
This book contains at least 10% recycled materials.

Library of Congress Cataloging-in-Publication Data

Gownley, Jimmy.
  Amelia in What makes you happy / Jimmy Gownley. -- Reinforced library bound ed.
    p. cm. -- (Jimmy Gownley's Amelia rules!)
  Summary: When Amelia finds a tape of an old song by her Aunt Tanner, a former rock star, she is not exactly sure what it means.
  ISBN 978-1-59961-792-3
  1. Graphic novels. [1. Graphic novels. 2. Aunts--Fiction. 3. Rock music--Fiction. 4. Secrets--Fiction.] I. Title. II. Title: What makes you happy.
  PZ7.7.G69Amw 2010
  741.5'973--dc22

                                                                    2010006193

All Spotlight books have reinforced library bindings and
are manufactured in the United States of America.

To my beautiful girls:
Stella Mary and
Anna Elizabeth,
And to their wonderful mother, Karen.

You're what make ME happy.

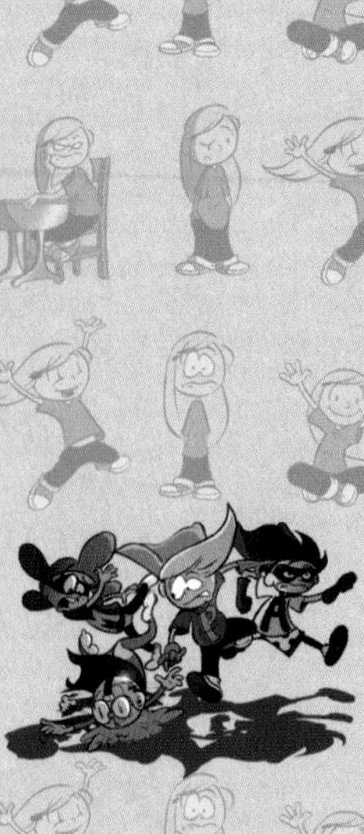

What Makes You Happy

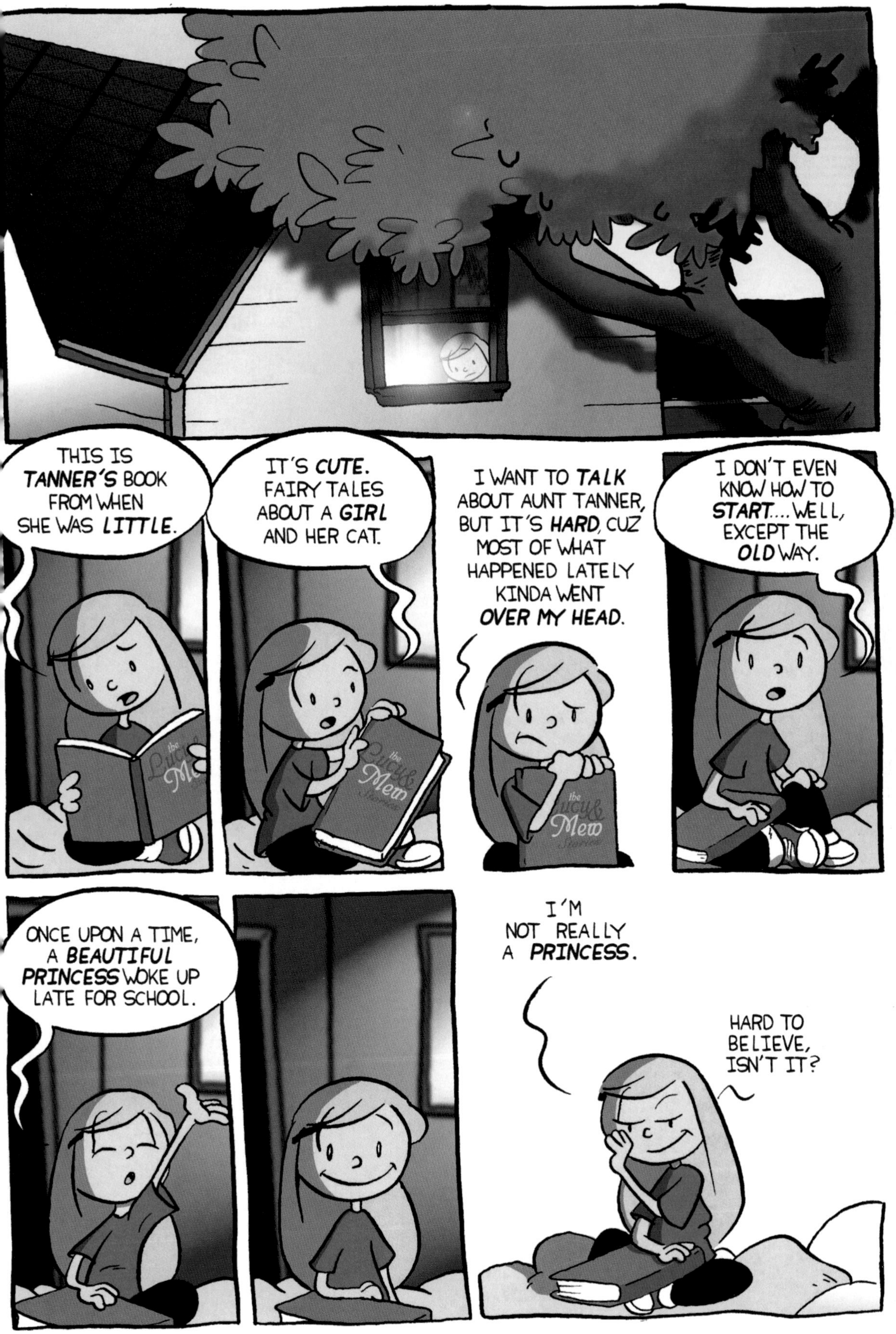
THIS IS TANNER'S BOOK FROM WHEN SHE WAS LITTLE.
IT'S CUTE. FAIRY TALES ABOUT A GIRL AND HER CAT.
the Lucy & Mew
I WANT TO TALK ABOUT AUNT TANNER, BUT IT'S HARD, CUZ MOST OF WHAT HAPPENED LATELY KINDA WENT OVER MY HEAD.
I DON'T EVEN KNOW HOW TO START.... WELL, EXCEPT THE OLD WAY.
ONCE UPON A TIME, A BEAUTIFUL PRINCESS WOKE UP LATE FOR SCHOOL.
I'M NOT REALLY A PRINCESS.
HARD TO BELIEVE, ISN'T IT?

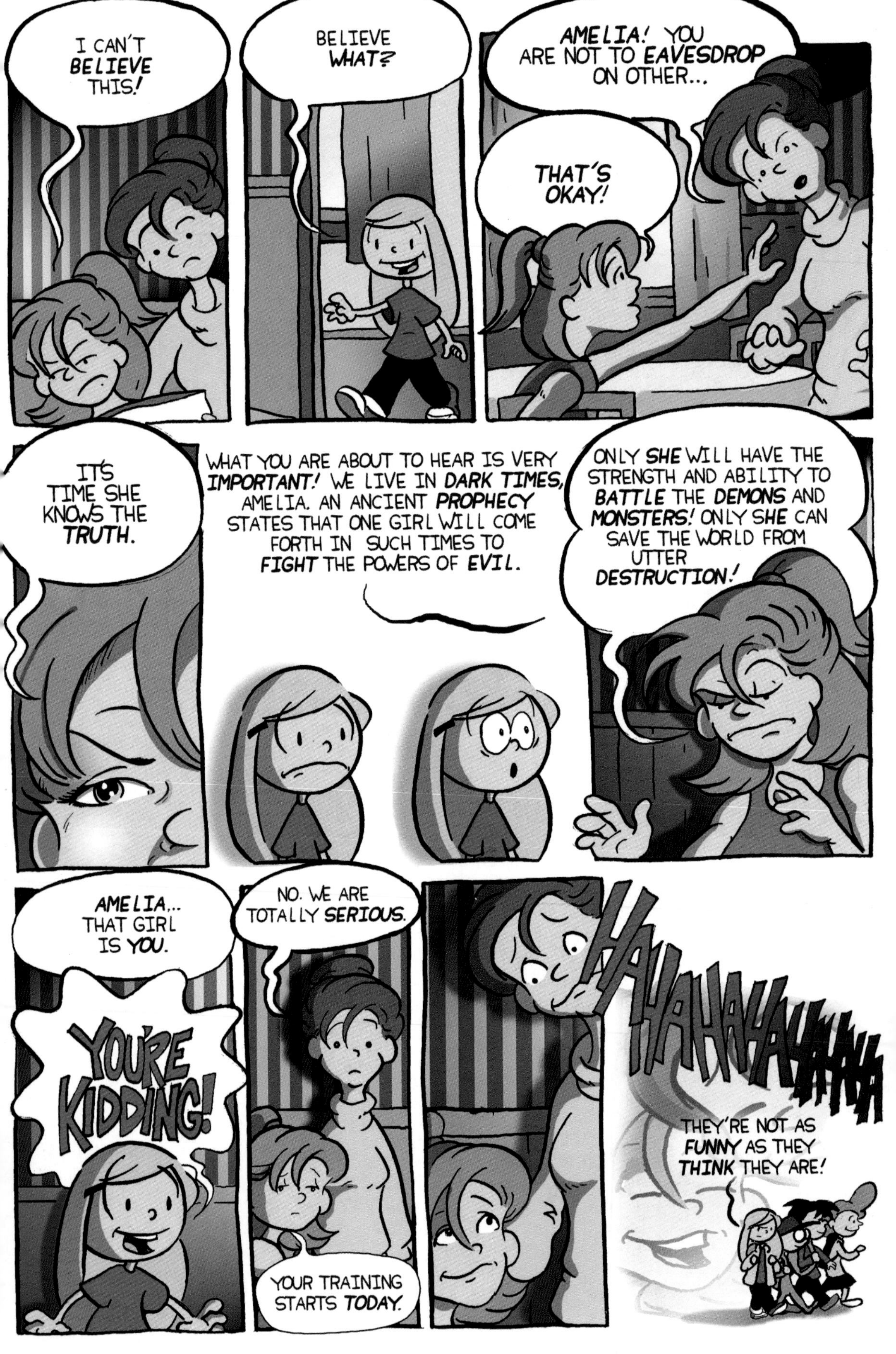
I CAN'T BELIEVE THIS!
BELIEVE WHAT?
AMELIA! YOU ARE NOT TO EAVESDROP ON OTHER...
THAT'S OKAY!
IT'S TIME SHE KNOWS THE TRUTH.
WHAT YOU ARE ABOUT TO HEAR IS VERY IMPORTANT! WE LIVE IN DARK TIMES, AMELIA. AN ANCIENT PROPHECY STATES THAT ONE GIRL WILL COME FORTH IN SUCH TIMES TO FIGHT THE POWERS OF EVIL.
ONLY SHE WILL HAVE THE STRENGTH AND ABILITY TO BATTLE THE DEMONS AND MONSTERS! ONLY SHE CAN SAVE THE WORLD FROM UTTER DESTRUCTION!
AMELIA... THAT GIRL IS YOU.
YOU'RE KIDDING!
NO. WE ARE TOTALLY SERIOUS.
YOUR TRAINING STARTS TODAY.
HAHAHAHAHAHAHAHA
THEY'RE NOT AS FUNNY AS THEY THINK THEY ARE!

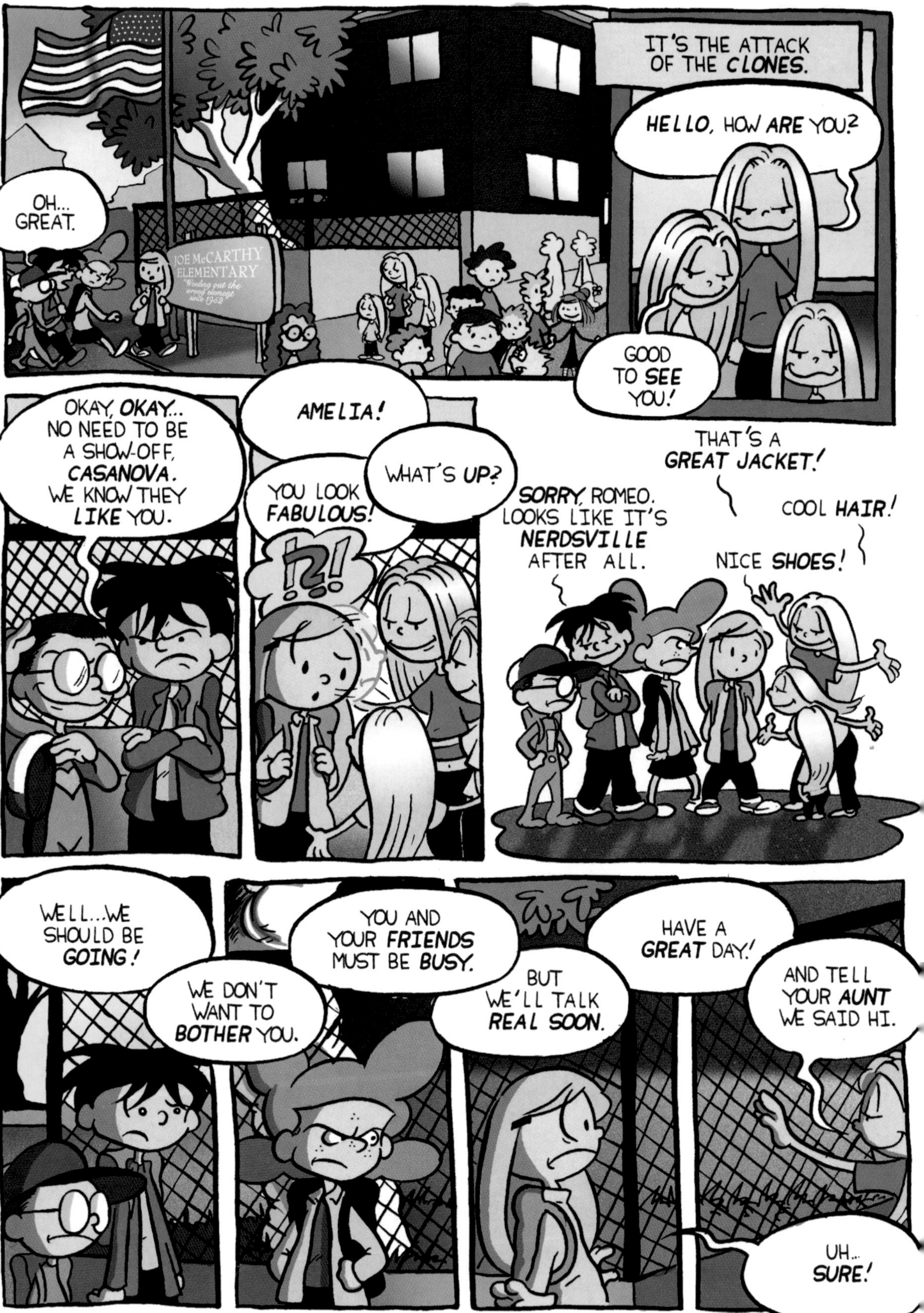
JOE McCARTHY ELEMENTARY
Weeding out the wrong element since 1952
OH... GREAT.
IT'S THE ATTACK OF THE CLONES.
HELLO, HOW ARE YOU?
GOOD TO SEE YOU!
OKAY, OKAY... NO NEED TO BE A SHOW-OFF, CASANOVA. WE KNOW THEY LIKE YOU.
AMELIA!
WHAT'S UP?
YOU LOOK FABULOUS!
?!
SORRY, ROMEO. LOOKS LIKE IT'S NERDSVILLE AFTER ALL.
THAT'S A GREAT JACKET!
COOL HAIR!
NICE SHOES!
WELL...WE SHOULD BE GOING!
WE DON'T WANT TO BOTHER YOU.
YOU AND YOUR FRIENDS MUST BE BUSY.
BUT WE'LL TALK REAL SOON.
HAVE A GREAT DAY!
AND TELL YOUR AUNT WE SAID HI.
UH... SURE!

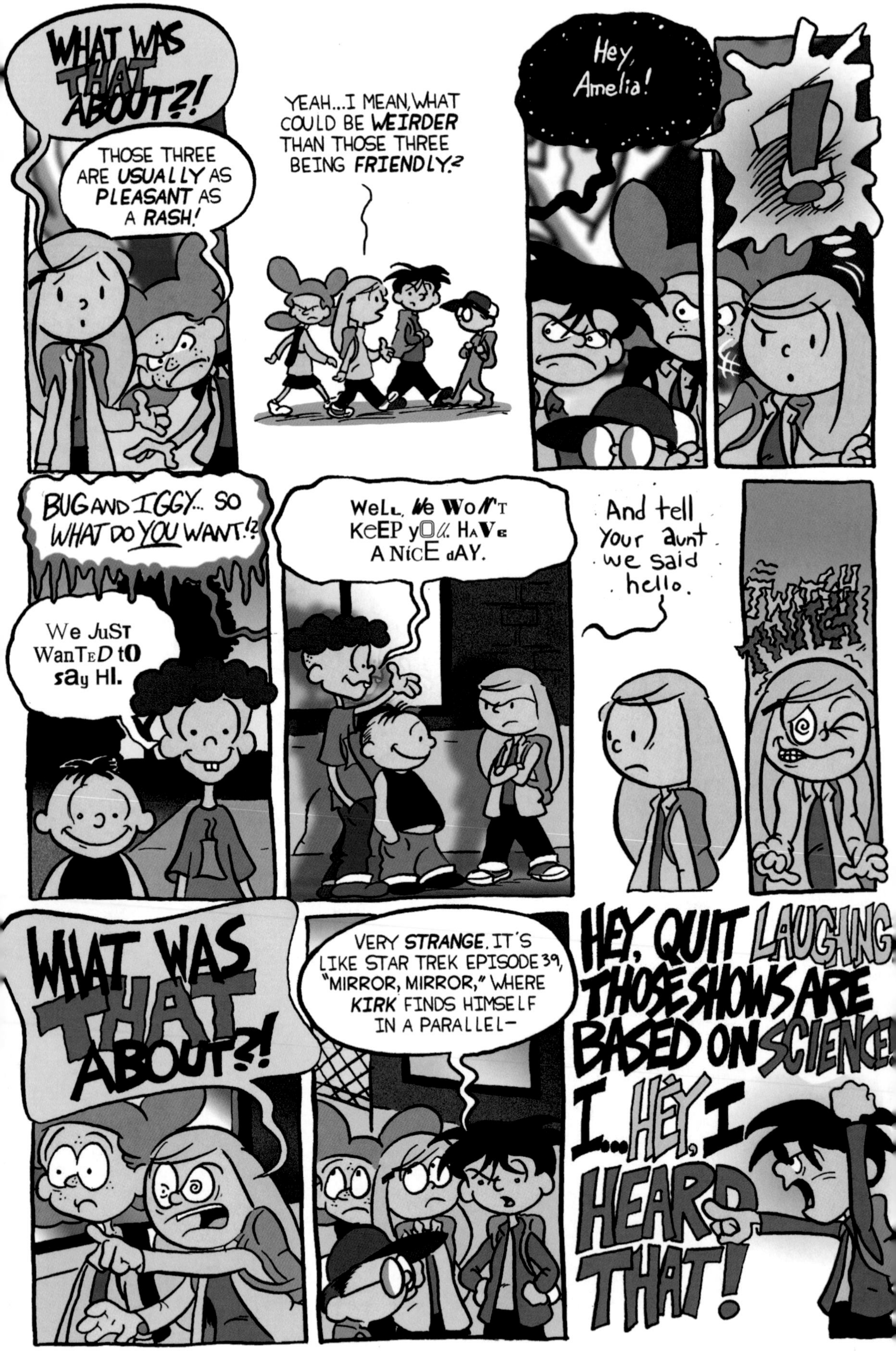
WHAT WAS THAT ABOUT?!
THOSE THREE ARE USUALLY AS PLEASANT AS A RASH!
YEAH...I MEAN, WHAT COULD BE WEIRDER THAN THOSE THREE BEING FRIENDLY?
Hey, Amelia!
!
BUG AND IGGY... SO WHAT DO YOU WANT!?
We JuST WanTeD tO say HI.
WeLL, We WoN'T KeEP yOU. HaVe A NicE dAY.
And tell your aunt we said hello.
TWITCH TWITCH
WHAT WAS THAT ABOUT?!
VERY STRANGE. IT'S LIKE STAR TREK EPISODE 39, "MIRROR, MIRROR," WHERE KIRK FINDS HIMSELF IN A PARALLEL—
HEY, QUIT LAUGHING THOSE SHOWS ARE BASED ON SCIENCE! I...HEY, I HEARD THAT!

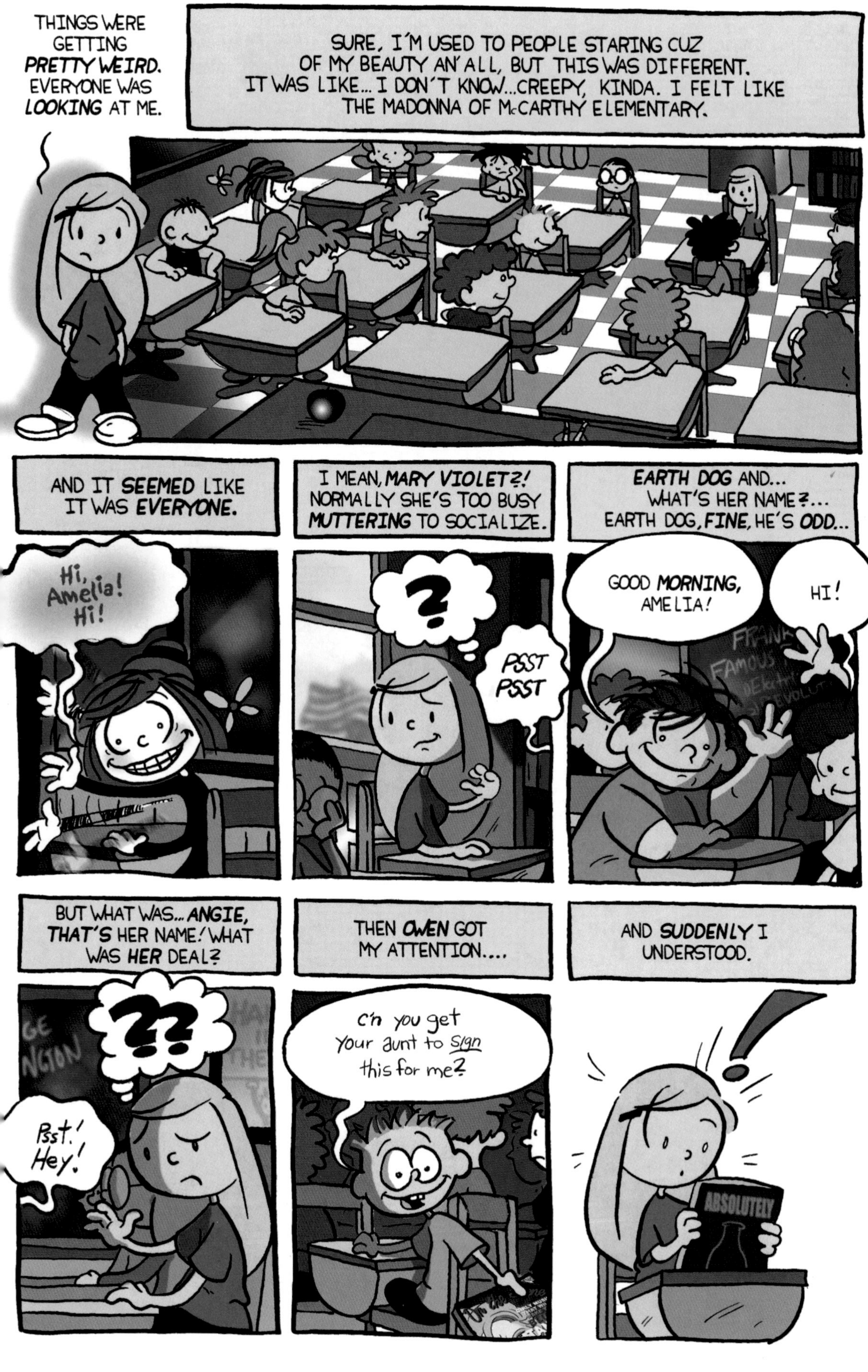
THINGS WERE GETTING PRETTY WEIRD. EVERYONE WAS LOOKING AT ME.
SURE, I'M USED TO PEOPLE STARING CUZ OF MY BEAUTY AN' ALL, BUT THIS WAS DIFFERENT. IT WAS LIKE... I DON'T KNOW...CREEPY, KINDA. I FELT LIKE THE MADONNA OF McCARTHY ELEMENTARY.
AND IT SEEMED LIKE IT WAS EVERYONE.
Hi, Amelia! Hi!
I MEAN, MARY VIOLET?! NORMALLY SHE'S TOO BUSY MUTTERING TO SOCIALIZE.
?
PSST PSST
EARTH DOG AND... WHAT'S HER NAME?... EARTH DOG, FINE, HE'S ODD...
GOOD MORNING, AMELIA!
HI!
BUT WHAT WAS... ANGIE, THAT'S HER NAME! WHAT WAS HER DEAL?
??
Psst! Hey!
THEN OWEN GOT MY ATTENTION....
c'n you get your aunt to sign this for me?
AND SUDDENLY I UNDERSTOOD.
!
ABSOLUTELY

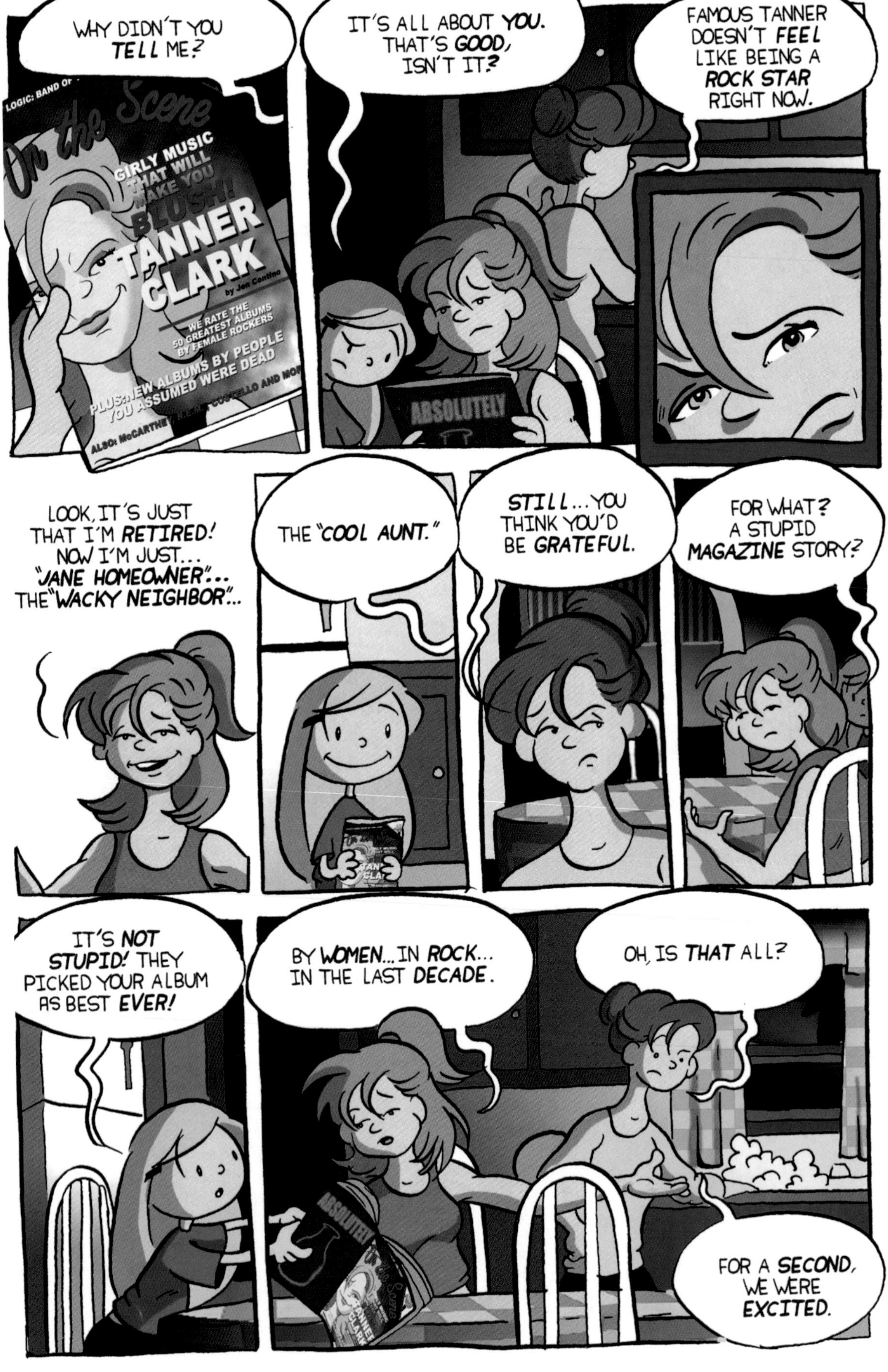
WHY DIDN'T YOU TELL ME?
On the Scene
GIRLY MUSIC THAT WILL MAKE YOU BLUSH!
TANNER CLARK
by Jen Contino
WE RATE THE 50 GREATEST ALBUMS BY FEMALE ROCKERS
PLUS: NEW ALBUMS BY PEOPLE YOU ASSUMED WERE DEAD
IT'S ALL ABOUT YOU. THAT'S GOOD, ISN'T IT?
ABSOLUTELY
FAMOUS TANNER DOESN'T FEEL LIKE BEING A ROCK STAR RIGHT NOW.
LOOK, IT'S JUST THAT I'M RETIRED! NOW I'M JUST... "JANE HOMEOWNER"... THE "WACKY NEIGHBOR"...
THE "COOL AUNT."
STILL... YOU THINK YOU'D BE GRATEFUL.
FOR WHAT? A STUPID MAGAZINE STORY?
IT'S NOT STUPID! THEY PICKED YOUR ALBUM AS BEST EVER!
BY WOMEN... IN ROCK... IN THE LAST DECADE.
OH, IS THAT ALL?
FOR A SECOND, WE WERE EXCITED.

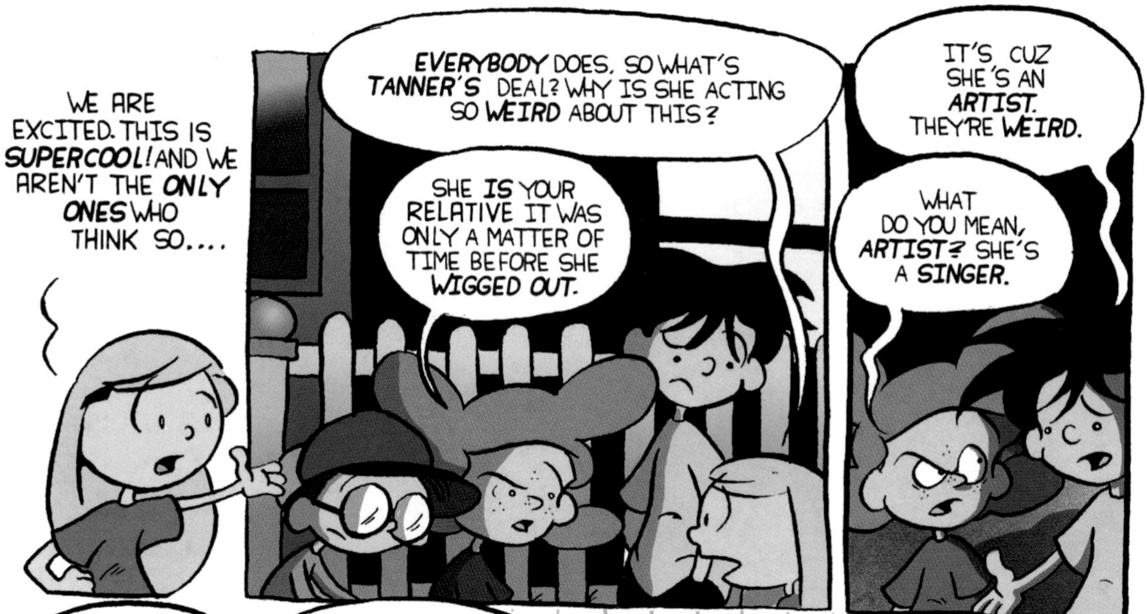
WE ARE EXCITED. THIS IS SUPERCOOL! AND WE AREN'T THE ONLY ONES WHO THINK SO....
EVERYBODY DOES. SO WHAT'S TANNER'S DEAL? WHY IS SHE ACTING SO WEIRD ABOUT THIS?
SHE IS YOUR RELATIVE. IT WAS ONLY A MATTER OF TIME BEFORE SHE WIGGED OUT.
IT'S CUZ SHE'S AN ARTIST. THEY'RE WEIRD.
WHAT DO YOU MEAN, ARTIST? SHE'S A SINGER.

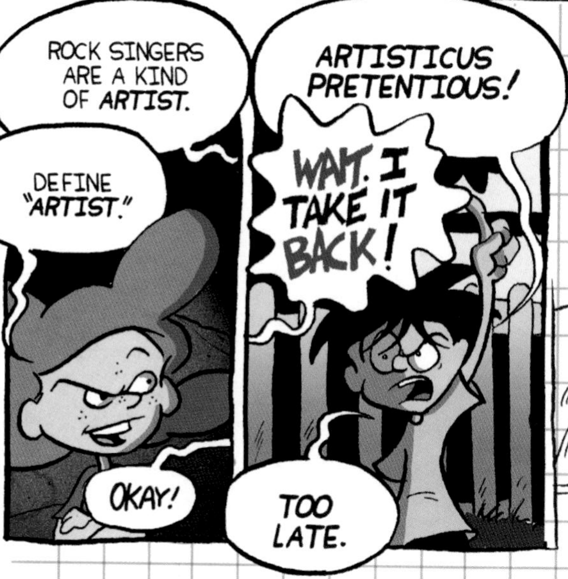
ROCK SINGERS ARE A KIND OF ARTIST.
DEFINE "ARTIST."
OKAY!
ARTISTICUS PRETENTIOUS!
WAIT. I TAKE IT BACK!
TOO LATE.

Artisticus Pretentious (the Common Artist) An artist is an individual who excels at any activity that is considered "art" (fig. 1). These activities can include, painting, poetry, sculpture, bowling, swearing, drooling, and essentially any field that is not "sales" or "comic books." Most of these individuals fall into the trap of learning "skills." This immediately disqualifies them from the title of "artists," and they become "hacks," or if they're the loud-mouthed type, "art directors." A true artist should have no skills, and if possible, the work should look as if it were done by a deranged toddler (fig. 2).

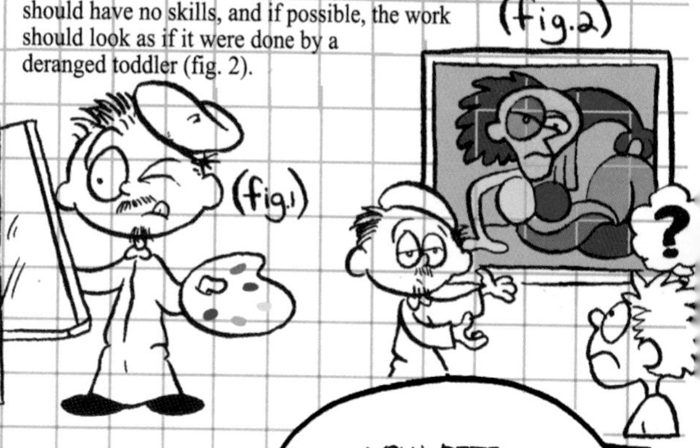
(fig.1)
(fig.2)
?

When an individual has reached the level of Artist, one of two things can occur. If that person can go on to create work that is loved by the masses and he or she reaps financial rewards from the work, then they become "sellouts" (fig. 3a). Males in this group are easy to spot, as they are the only artists ever to be seen with girls. Or the artist might be lucky and receive no credit, money, success, or attention, thereby guaranteeing themselves recognition as a "great artist" (fig. 3b). For these fortunate few, the only step left is to be declared a genius. This is easily accomplished by dying a stupid, preventable death, or by severing a body part and sending it to a loved one (fig. 4).

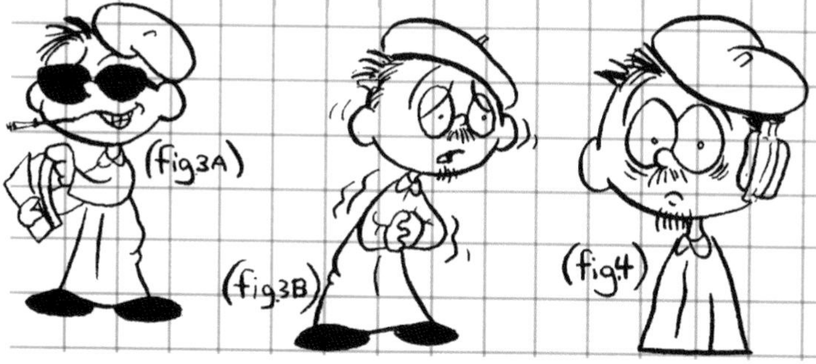
(fig3A)
(fig3B)
(fig4)

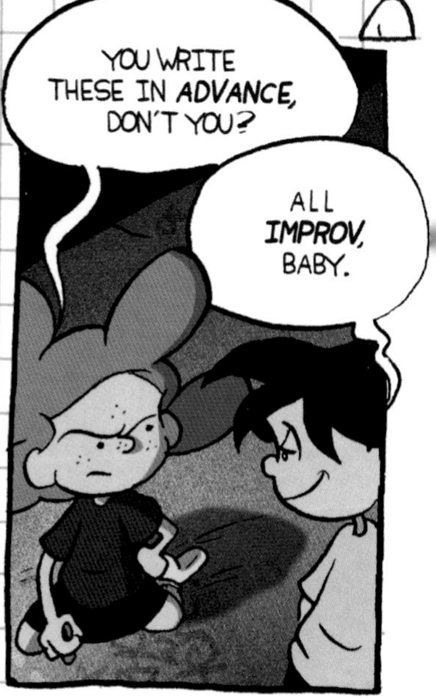
YOU WRITE THESE IN ADVANCE, DON'T YOU?
ALL IMPROV, BABY.

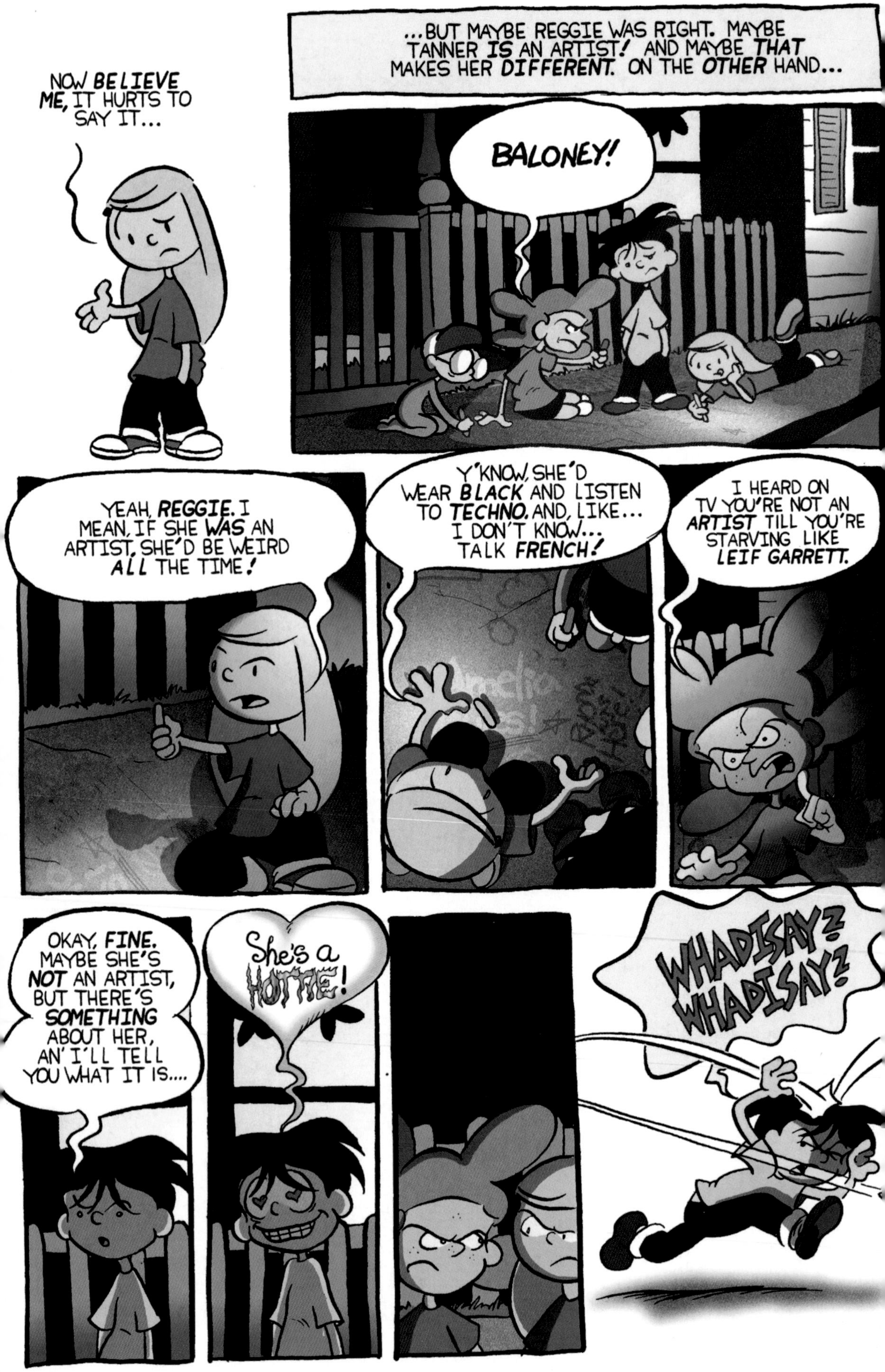
NOW BELIEVE ME, IT HURTS TO SAY IT...
...BUT MAYBE REGGIE WAS RIGHT. MAYBE TANNER IS AN ARTIST! AND MAYBE THAT MAKES HER DIFFERENT. ON THE OTHER HAND...
BALONEY!
YEAH, REGGIE. I MEAN, IF SHE WAS AN ARTIST, SHE'D BE WEIRD ALL THE TIME!
Y'KNOW, SHE'D WEAR BLACK AND LISTEN TO TECHNO. AND, LIKE... I DON'T KNOW... TALK FRENCH!
I HEARD ON TV YOU'RE NOT AN ARTIST TILL YOU'RE STARVING LIKE LEIF GARRETT.
OKAY, FINE. MAYBE SHE'S NOT AN ARTIST, BUT THERE'S SOMETHING ABOUT HER, AN' I'LL TELL YOU WHAT IT IS....
She's a HOTTIE!
WHADISAY? WHADISAY?

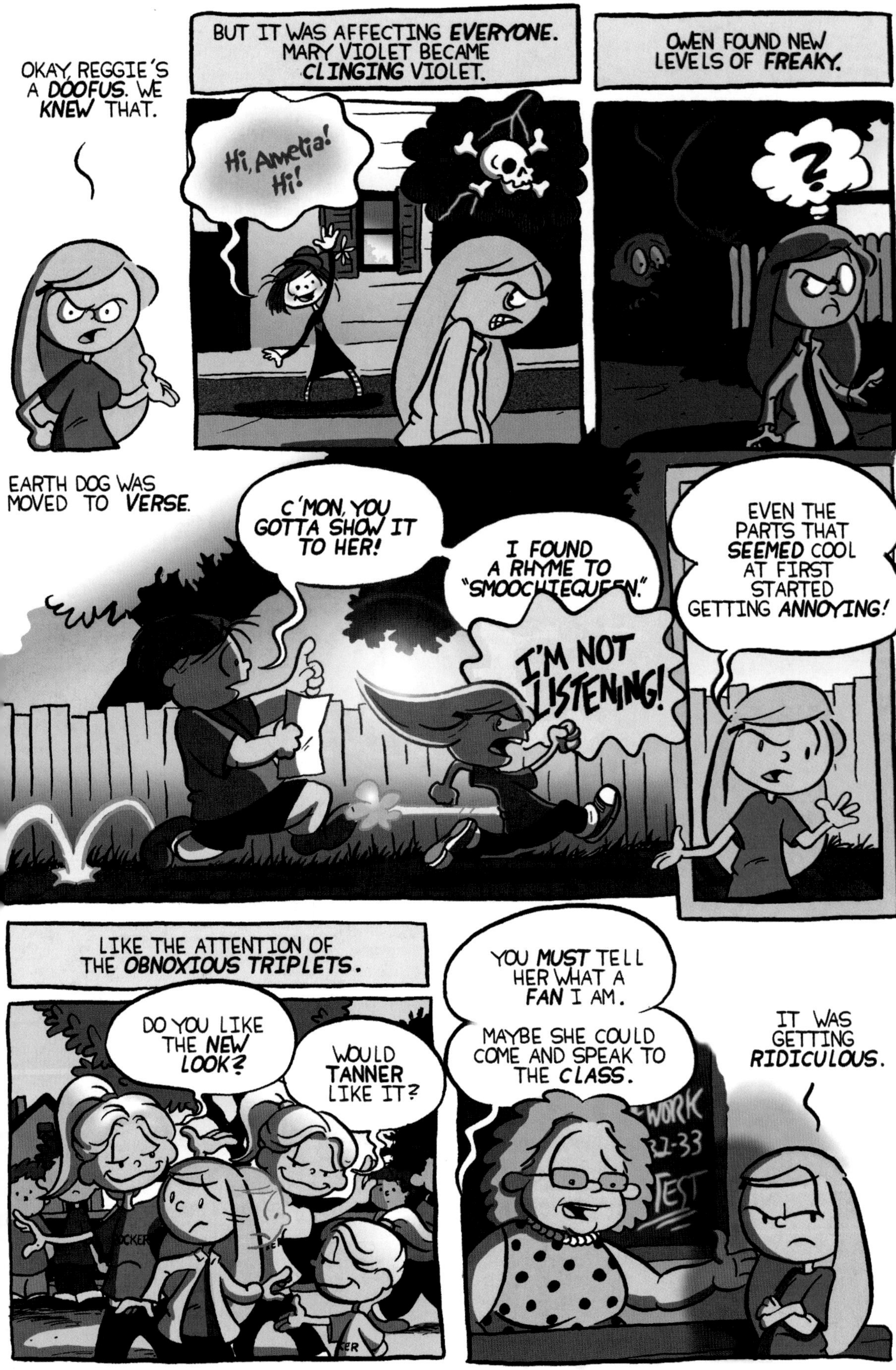
OKAY, REGGIE'S A DOOFUS. WE KNEW THAT.
BUT IT WAS AFFECTING EVERYONE. MARY VIOLET BECAME CLINGING VIOLET.
Hi, Amelia! Hi!
OWEN FOUND NEW LEVELS OF FREAKY.
?
EARTH DOG WAS MOVED TO VERSE.
C'MON, YOU GOTTA SHOW IT TO HER!
I FOUND A RHYME TO "SMOOCHIEQUEEN."
I'M NOT LISTENING!
EVEN THE PARTS THAT SEEMED COOL AT FIRST STARTED GETTING ANNOYING!
LIKE THE ATTENTION OF THE OBNOXIOUS TRIPLETS.
DO YOU LIKE THE NEW LOOK?
WOULD TANNER LIKE IT?
YOU MUST TELL HER WHAT A FAN I AM.
MAYBE SHE COULD COME AND SPEAK TO THE CLASS.
IT WAS GETTING RIDICULOUS.

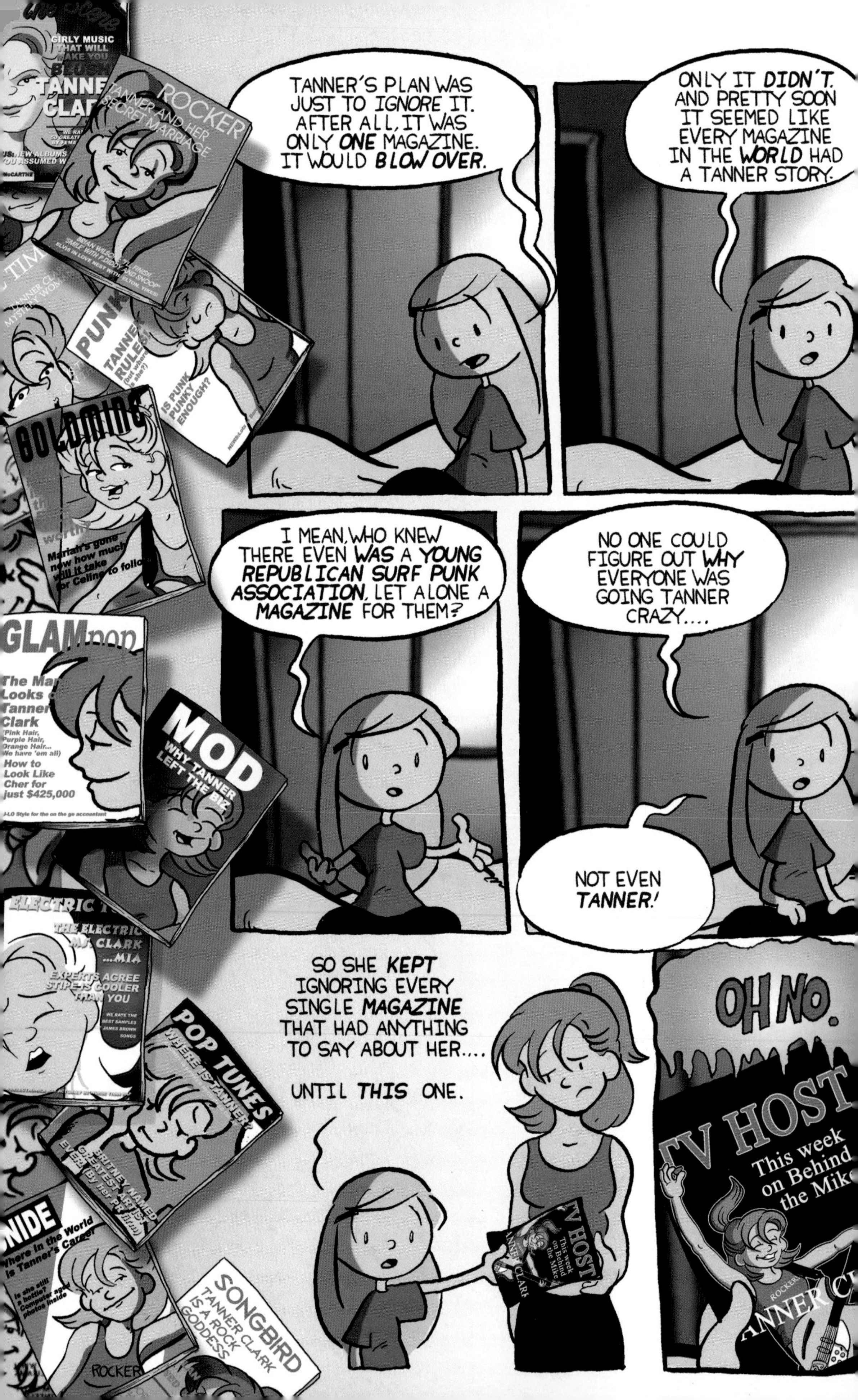
TANNER'S PLAN WAS JUST TO IGNORE IT. AFTER ALL, IT WAS ONLY ONE MAGAZINE. IT WOULD BLOW OVER.
ONLY IT DIDN'T. AND PRETTY SOON IT SEEMED LIKE EVERY MAGAZINE IN THE WORLD HAD A TANNER STORY.
I MEAN, WHO KNEW THERE EVEN WAS A YOUNG REPUBLICAN SURF PUNK ASSOCIATION, LET ALONE A MAGAZINE FOR THEM?
NO ONE COULD FIGURE OUT WHY EVERYONE WAS GOING TANNER CRAZY....
NOT EVEN TANNER!
SO SHE KEPT IGNORING EVERY SINGLE MAGAZINE THAT HAD ANYTHING TO SAY ABOUT HER....
UNTIL THIS ONE.
OH NO.
TV HOST
This week on Behind the Mike
GIRLY MUSIC THAT WILL MAKE YOU BLUSH
ROCKER
TANNER AND HER SECRET MARRIAGE
PUNK
TANNER RULES!
IS PUNK PUNKY ENOUGH?
GOLDMINE
Mariah's gone now how much will it take for Celine to follow
GLAMpop
How to Look Like Cher for just $425,000
J-LO Style for the on the go accountant
MOD
WHY TANNER LEFT THE BIZ
EXPERTS AGREE STIPE IS COOLER THAN YOU
POP TUNES
WHERE IS TANNER?
Where in the World is Tanner's Career
SONGBIRD
TANNER CLARK IS A ROCK GODDESS

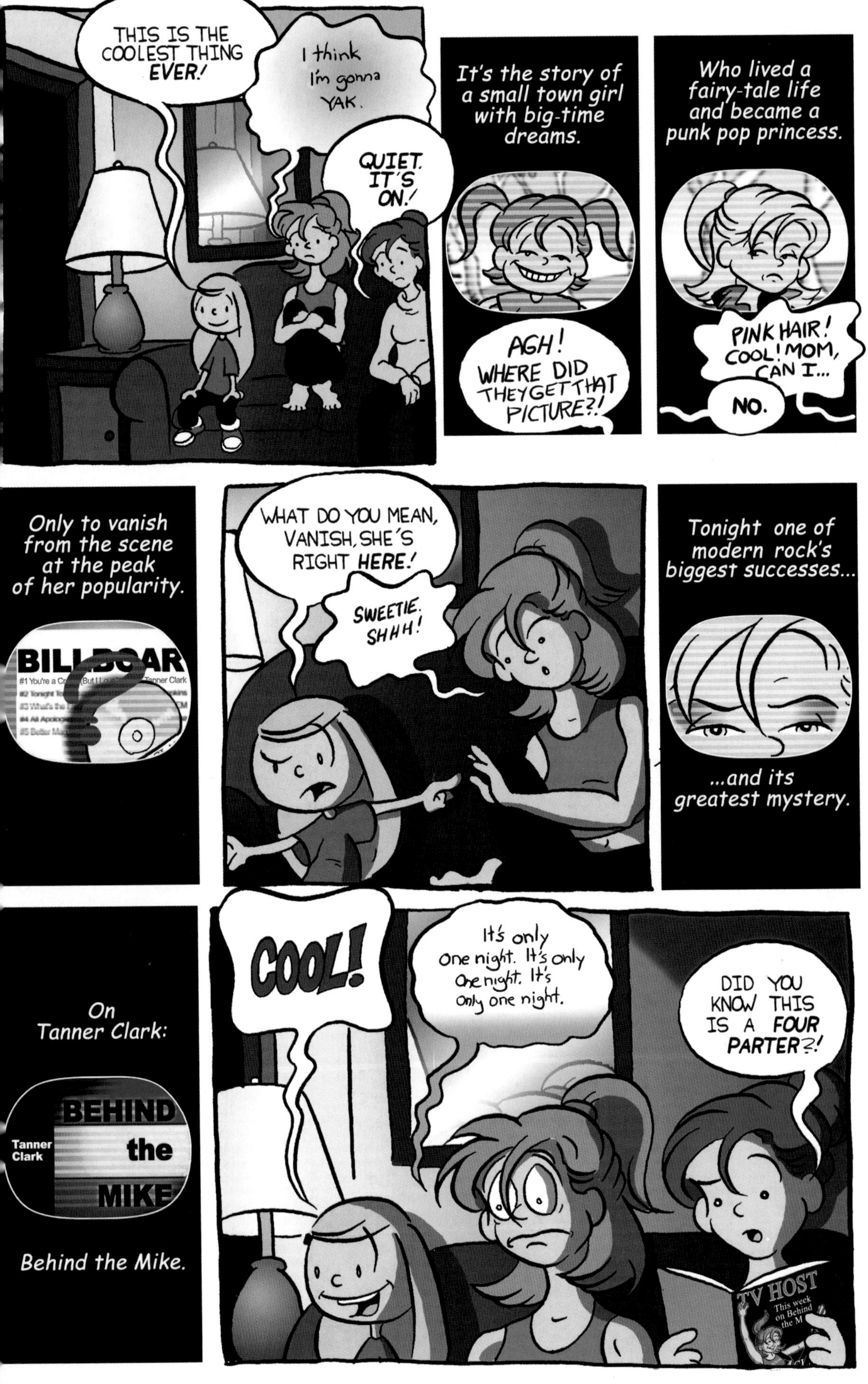
THIS IS THE COOLEST THING EVER!
I think I'm gonna YAK.
QUIET. IT'S ON!
It's the story of a small town girl with big-time dreams.
AGH! WHERE DID THEY GET THAT PICTURE?!
Who lived a fairy-tale life and became a punk pop princess.
PINK HAIR! COOL! MOM, CAN I...
NO.
Only to vanish from the scene at the peak of her popularity.
BILLBOAR
WHAT DO YOU MEAN, VANISH, SHE'S RIGHT HERE!
SWEETIE. SHHH!
Tonight one of modern rock's biggest successes...
...and its greatest mystery.
On Tanner Clark:
Tanner Clark
BEHIND the MIKE
Behind the Mike.
COOL!
It's only one night. It's only one night. It's only one night.
DID YOU KNOW THIS IS A FOUR PARTER?!
TV HOST
This week on Behind the M

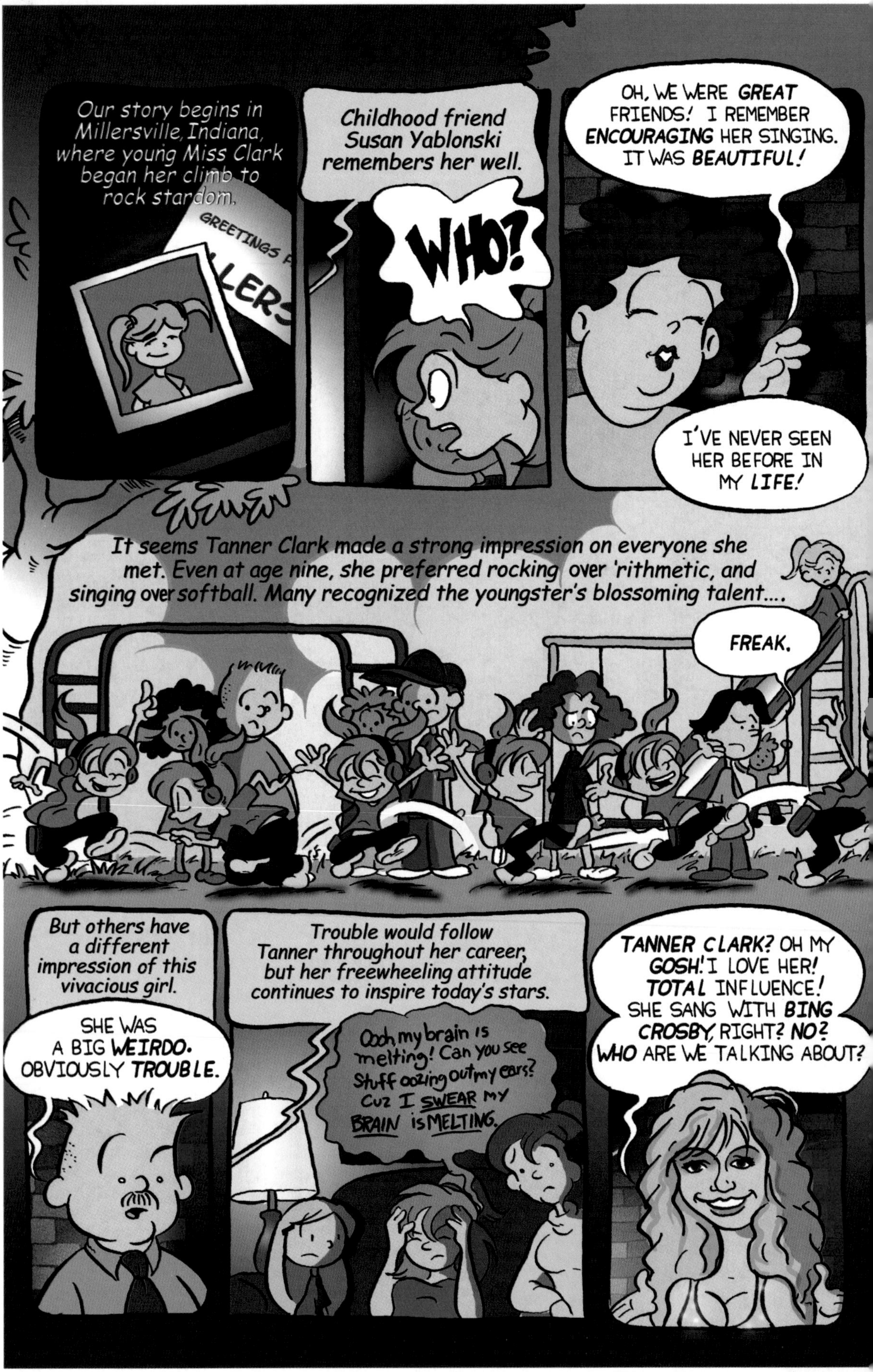
Our story begins in Millersville, Indiana, where young Miss Clark began her climb to rock stardom.
GREETINGS F
LLERS
Childhood friend Susan Yablonski remembers her well.
WHO?
OH, WE WERE GREAT FRIENDS! I REMEMBER ENCOURAGING HER SINGING. IT WAS BEAUTIFUL!
I'VE NEVER SEEN HER BEFORE IN MY LIFE!
It seems Tanner Clark made a strong impression on everyone she met. Even at age nine, she preferred rocking over 'rithmetic, and singing over softball. Many recognized the youngster's blossoming talent....
FREAK.
But others have a different impression of this vivacious girl.
SHE WAS A BIG WEIRDO. OBVIOUSLY TROUBLE.
Trouble would follow Tanner throughout her career, but her freewheeling attitude continues to inspire today's stars.
Oooh, my brain is melting! Can you see stuff oozing out my ears? Cuz I SWEAR my BRAIN is MELTING.
TANNER CLARK? OH MY GOSH! I LOVE HER! TOTAL INFLUENCE! SHE SANG WITH BING CROSBY, RIGHT? NO? WHO ARE WE TALKING ABOUT?

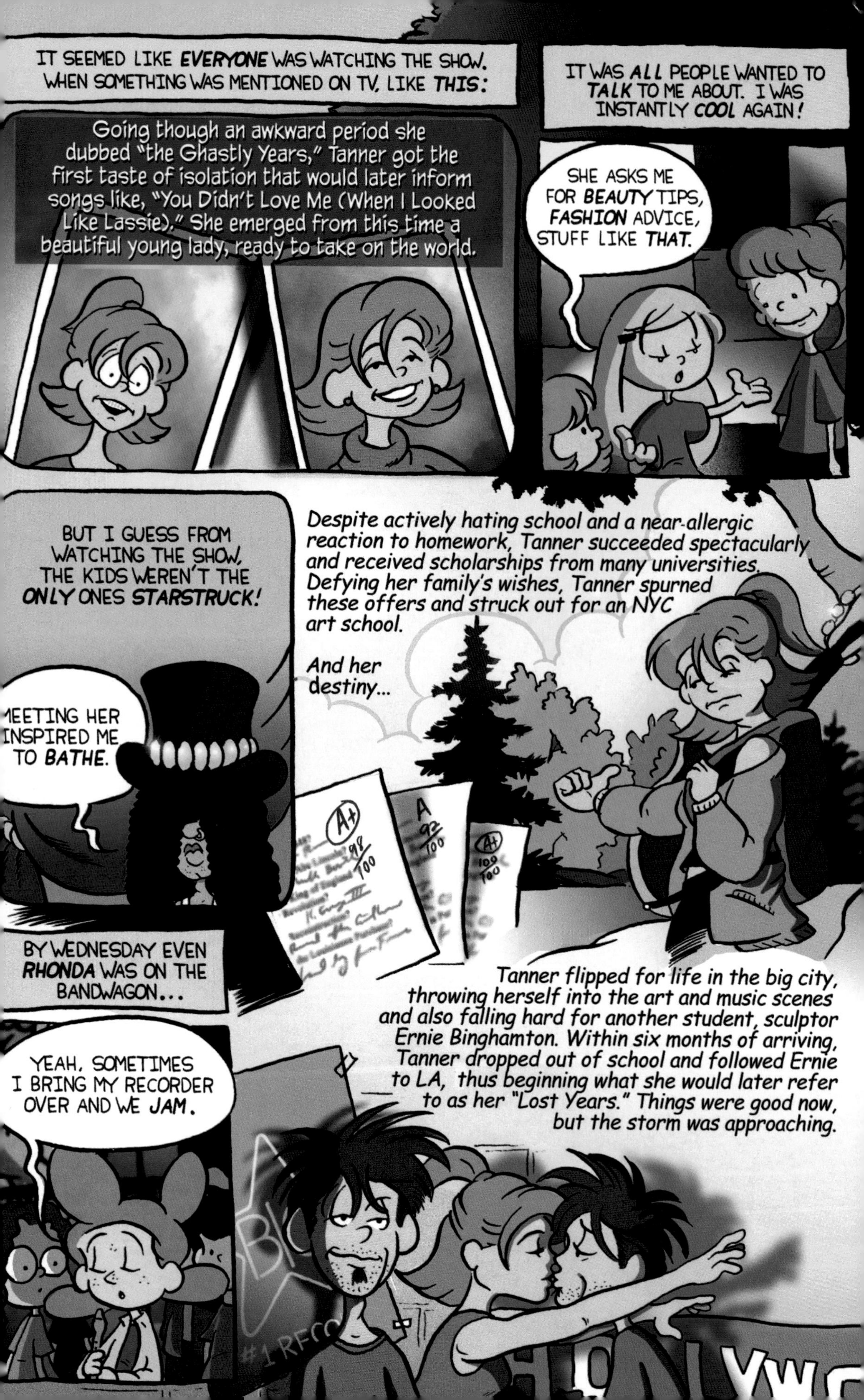
IT SEEMED LIKE EVERYONE WAS WATCHING THE SHOW. WHEN SOMETHING WAS MENTIONED ON TV, LIKE THIS:
Going though an awkward period she dubbed "the Ghastly Years," Tanner got the first taste of isolation that would later inform songs like, "You Didn't Love Me (When I Looked Like Lassie)." She emerged from this time a beautiful young lady, ready to take on the world.
IT WAS ALL PEOPLE WANTED TO TALK TO ME ABOUT. I WAS INSTANTLY COOL AGAIN!
SHE ASKS ME FOR BEAUTY TIPS, FASHION ADVICE, STUFF LIKE THAT.
BUT I GUESS FROM WATCHING THE SHOW, THE KIDS WEREN'T THE ONLY ONES STARSTRUCK!
MEETING HER INSPIRED ME TO BATHE.
BY WEDNESDAY EVEN RHONDA WAS ON THE BANDWAGON...
YEAH, SOMETIMES I BRING MY RECORDER OVER AND WE JAM.
Despite actively hating school and a near-allergic reaction to homework, Tanner succeeded spectacularly and received scholarships from many universities. Defying her family's wishes, Tanner spurned these offers and struck out for an NYC art school.
And her destiny...
A+ 98/100
A 92/100
A+ 100/100
Tanner flipped for life in the big city, throwing herself into the art and music scenes and also falling hard for another student, sculptor Ernie Binghamton. Within six months of arriving, Tanner dropped out of school and followed Ernie to LA, thus beginning what she would later refer to as her "Lost Years." Things were good now, but the storm was approaching.

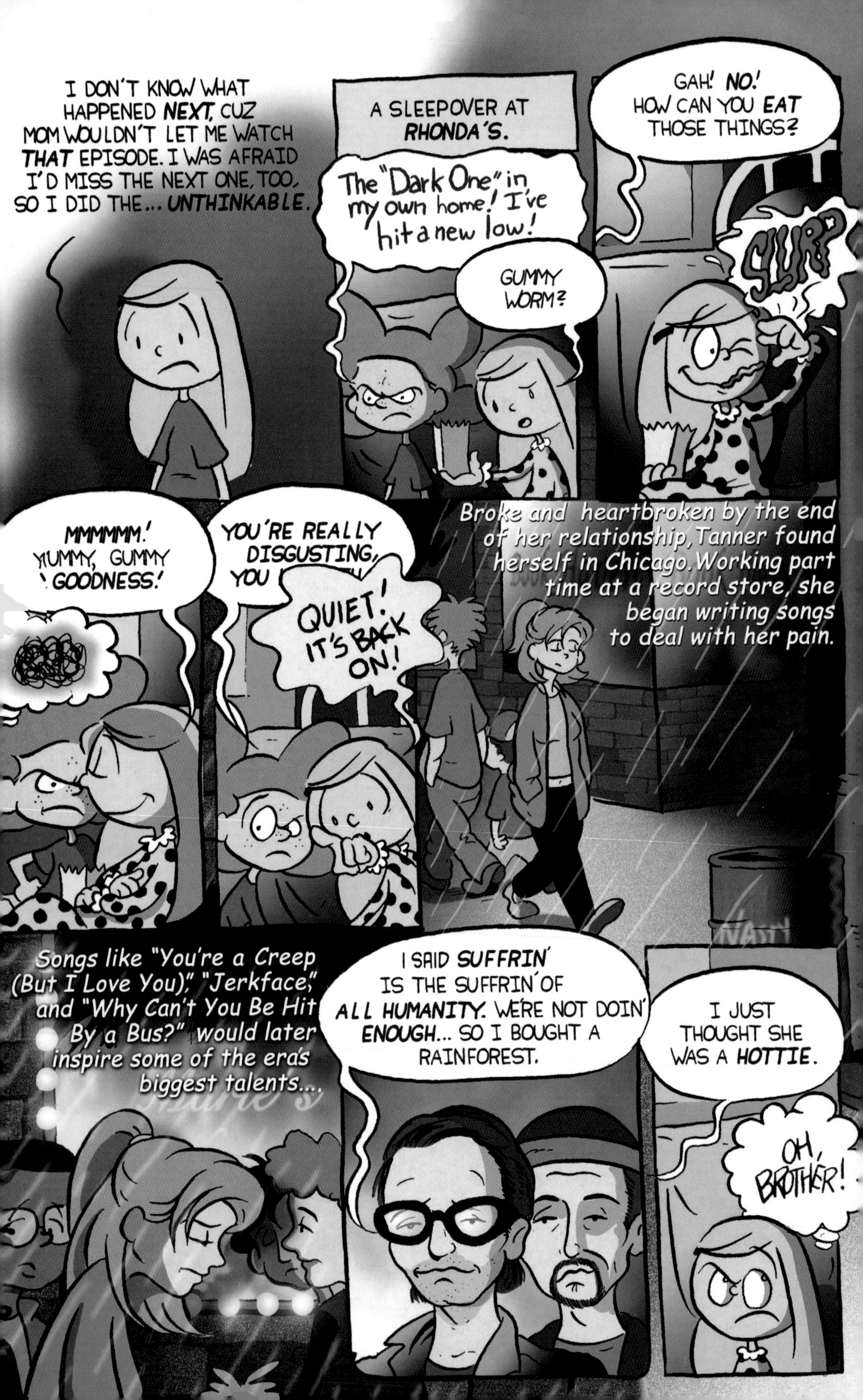
I DON'T KNOW WHAT HAPPENED NEXT, CUZ MOM WOULDN'T LET ME WATCH THAT EPISODE. I WAS AFRAID I'D MISS THE NEXT ONE, TOO, SO I DID THE... UNTHINKABLE.
A SLEEPOVER AT RHONDA'S.
The "Dark One" in my own home! I've hit a new low!
GUMMY WORM?
GAH! NO! HOW CAN YOU EAT THOSE THINGS?
SLURP
MMMMMM! YUMMY, GUMMY GOODNESS!
YOU'RE REALLY DISGUSTING, YOU
QUIET! IT'S BACK ON!
Broke and heartbroken by the end of her relationship, Tanner found herself in Chicago. Working part time at a record store, she began writing songs to deal with her pain.
Songs like "You're a Creep (But I Love You)," "Jerkface," and "Why Can't You Be Hit By a Bus?" would later inspire some of the era's biggest talents...
I SAID SUFFRIN' IS THE SUFFRIN' OF ALL HUMANITY. WE'RE NOT DOIN' ENOUGH... SO I BOUGHT A RAINFOREST.
I JUST THOUGHT SHE WAS A HOTTIE.
OH, BROTHER!

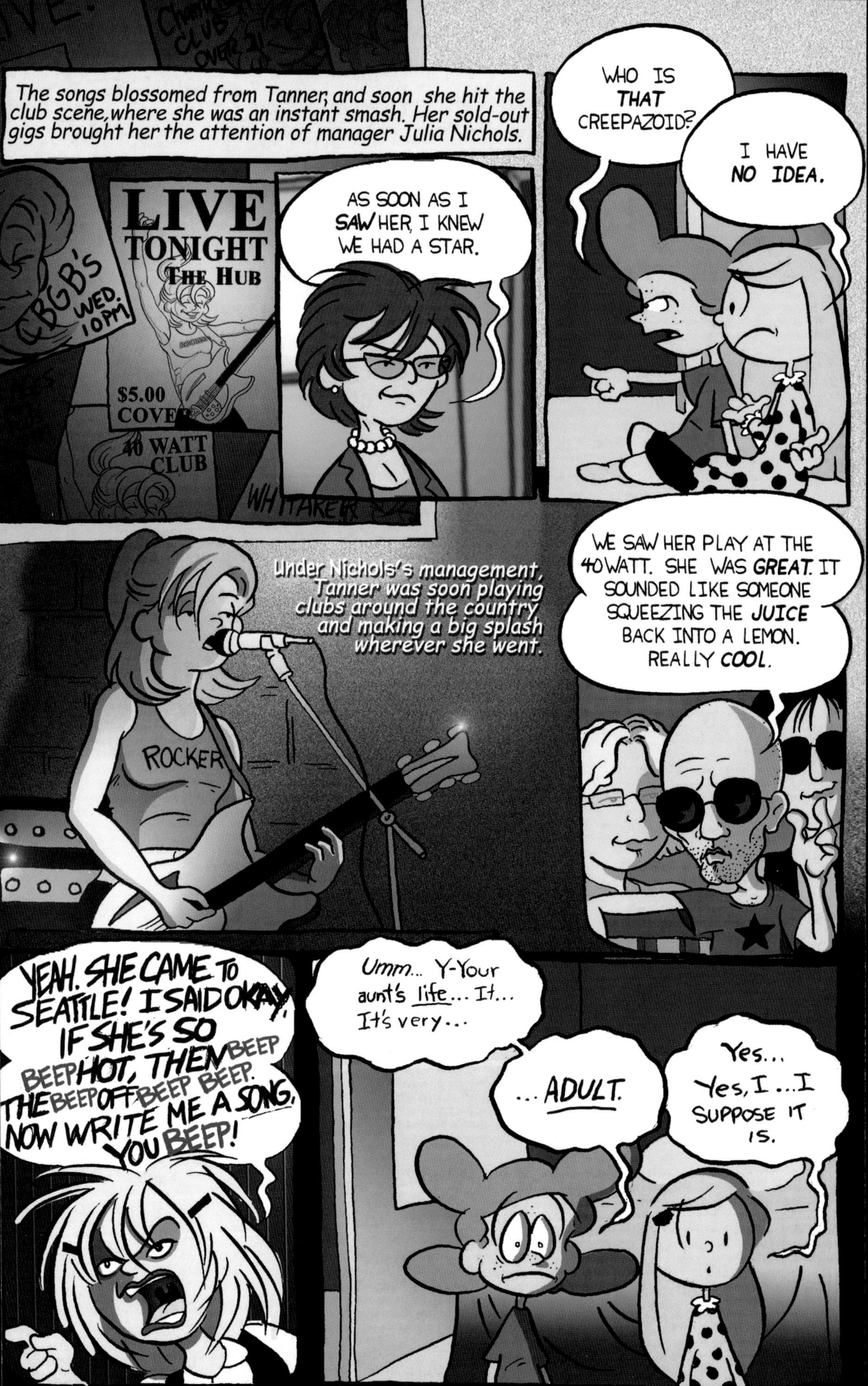
The songs blossomed from Tanner, and soon she hit the club scene, where she was an instant smash. Her sold-out gigs brought her the attention of manager Julia Nichols.
LIVE TONIGHT THE HUB
CBGB's WED. 10PM
$5.00 COVER
40 WATT CLUB
AS SOON AS I SAW HER, I KNEW WE HAD A STAR.
WHO IS THAT CREEPAZOID?
I HAVE NO IDEA.
Under Nichols's management, Tanner was soon playing clubs around the country and making a big splash wherever she went.
ROCKER
WE SAW HER PLAY AT THE 40 WATT. SHE WAS GREAT. IT SOUNDED LIKE SOMEONE SQUEEZING THE JUICE BACK INTO A LEMON. REALLY COOL.
YEAH. SHE CAME TO SEATTLE! I SAID OKAY, IF SHE'S SO BEEP HOT, THEN BEEP THE BEEP OFF BEEP BEEP. NOW WRITE ME A SONG, YOU BEEP!
Umm... Y-Your aunt's life... It... It's very...
...ADULT.
Yes... Yes, I...I suppose it is.

I GUESS MOM FIGURED THE LAST EPISODE WOULD BE **TAME,** SO SHE LET ME WATCH IT AT **HOME**. NOT THAT ANY OF US GOT TO **SEE** MUCH, ANYWAY.

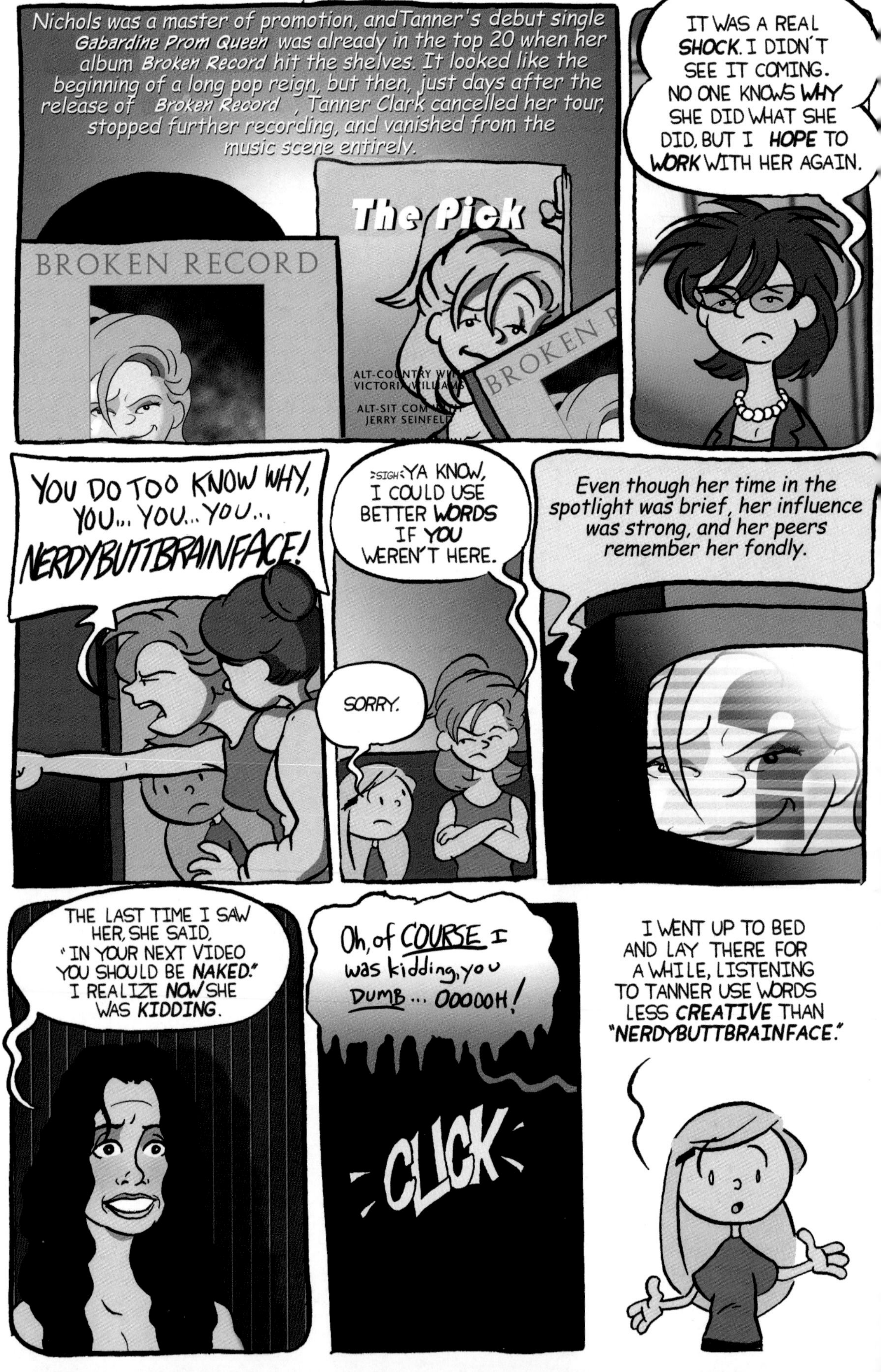

Nichols was a master of promotion, and Tanner's debut single Gabardine Prom Queen was already in the top 20 when her album Broken Record hit the shelves. It looked like the beginning of a long pop reign, but then, just days after the release of Broken Record, Tanner Clark cancelled her tour, stopped further recording, and vanished from the music scene entirely.
BROKEN RECORD
The Pick
IT WAS A REAL SHOCK. I DIDN'T SEE IT COMING. NO ONE KNOWS WHY SHE DID WHAT SHE DID, BUT I HOPE TO WORK WITH HER AGAIN.
YOU DO TOO KNOW WHY, YOU... YOU... YOU... NERDYBUTTBRAINFACE!
SIGH: YA KNOW, I COULD USE BETTER WORDS IF YOU WEREN'T HERE.
SORRY.
Even though her time in the spotlight was brief, her influence was strong, and her peers remember her fondly.
THE LAST TIME I SAW HER, SHE SAID, "IN YOUR NEXT VIDEO YOU SHOULD BE NAKED." I REALIZE NOW SHE WAS KIDDING.
Oh, of COURSE I was kidding, you DUMB... OOOOOH!
CLICK
I WENT UP TO BED AND LAY THERE FOR A WHILE, LISTENING TO TANNER USE WORDS LESS CREATIVE THAN "NERDYBUTTBRAINFACE."

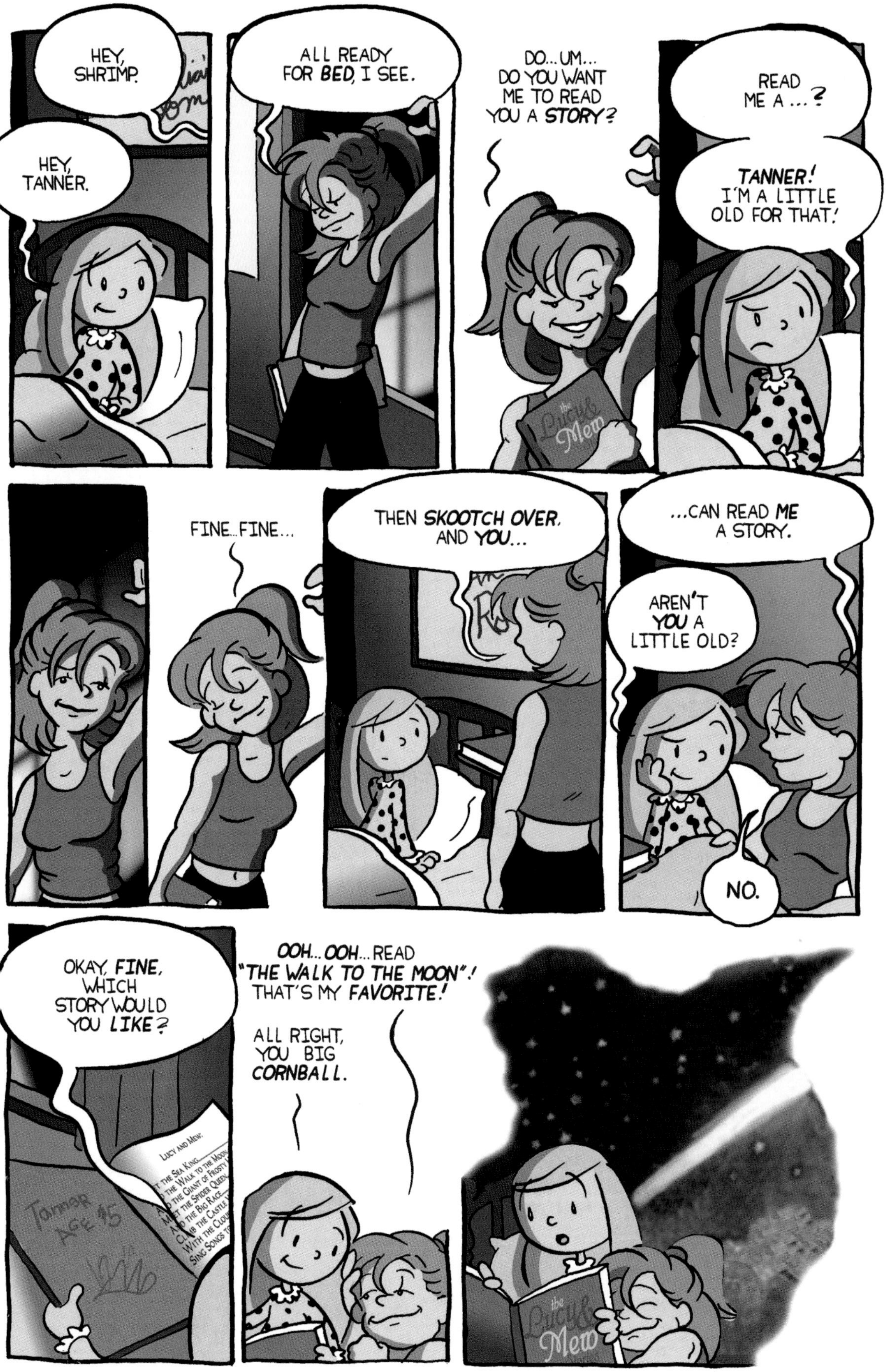
HEY, SHRIMP.
HEY, TANNER.
ALL READY FOR BED, I SEE.
DO... UM... DO YOU WANT ME TO READ YOU A STORY?
READ ME A ...?
TANNER! I'M A LITTLE OLD FOR THAT!
FINE...FINE...
THEN SKOOTCH OVER, AND YOU...
...CAN READ ME A STORY.
AREN'T YOU A LITTLE OLD?
NO.
OKAY, FINE, WHICH STORY WOULD YOU LIKE?
OOH... OOH... READ "THE WALK TO THE MOON"! THAT'S MY FAVORITE!
ALL RIGHT, YOU BIG CORNBALL.

The Walk to the Moon

by Beth Ellen Welch

Once upon a time there was a poor young girl named Lucy who lived with a cat named Mew. Lucy and Mew lived in a very small house in a very small village in an enormous country that probably never existed, but which seemed quite nice. Lucy had no parents, and so she relied on Mew to care for her. This was not a problem, for Mew was a talented cat and earned more than many of the men in the village, and even as much as a few of the more prominent sheep. In exchange for her keep, Lucy kept the house tidy, the food and water dishes full, and the litter box clean. But Lucy was bored.

"There's nothing ever to do in this village," she complained to Mew. "I've heard other girls speak of villages with many dwellings under one roof, staircases that carry you magically from floor to floor, and merchants with goods from faraway lands; shops of all kinds selling fragrances, literature, garments, and equipment for sport, a common area where people may sample morsels and delicacies from all the world over. And outside yet another dining hall, set under glorious, illuminated golden arches."

"My business dealings have taken me to such villages," said Mew. "The people seem no happier there than they do any place else on Earth."

It was then that Lucy had a brilliant idea.

"But what about off the Earth?" she cried. "What about the village on the moon!" Mew had to admit that he had never heard of such villages, but still he was intrigued. "I imagine a cat with my skills in accounting could make as good a living on the moon as in this village," he said. And so Lucy and Mew decided to walk to the moon.

The plan was simple: Wait until the next rainbow appeared, walk to the top, then jump the remaining distance to the moon. "A brilliant plan," said Mew. "It's a wonder no one has thought of it before."

The two travelers took nothing with them save Lucy's umbrella and a large roll of cash. Everything they needed, they reasoned, they would get in the wondrous moon village.

The trip was longer than they expected, and Mew was very cross at Lucy for not having thought to bring even a small can of tuna. Lucy's legs got tired, but she sustained herself by thinking of the wonders the moon village were sure to contain.

Finally, the top of the rainbow was reached. The leap was taken, and Lucy and Mew landed on the moon. They were so happy to have arrived that they danced as only an orphan girl and her benefactor cat can dance.

Unfortunately, after celebrating, they realized

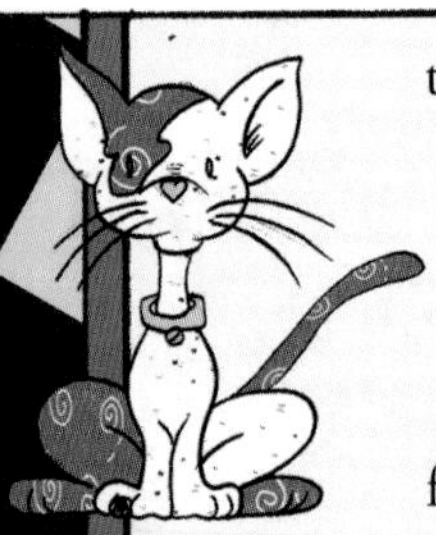

there was not a village in sight. "I'm sure they are here," said Lucy. "We just need to explore a bit."

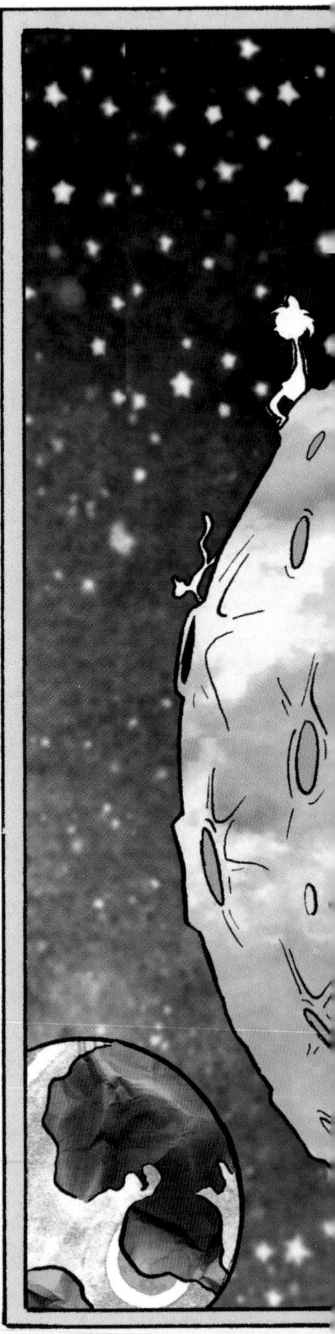

But after hours and days and weeks of exploring, all Lucy and Mew had found were some flags, a sculpture, and a carriage (but no horse).

"This is terrible!" cried Lucy. "We're completely alone!"

"We're never alone if we have each other," said Mew.

"Oh, shut up," said Lucy.

With nothing to do but sit on the rim of a crater and stare at Earth, Lucy and Mew both became melancholy.

"I miss having a home to clean and dishes to fill, and, well . . . maybe not the litter box," said Lucy.

"I'm just glad that cheese thing turned out to be true," said Mew. "Otherwise we would have starved."

Lucy decided that enough was enough, and, grabbing Mew with one hand and her umbrella with the other, she leaped off the edge of the moon.

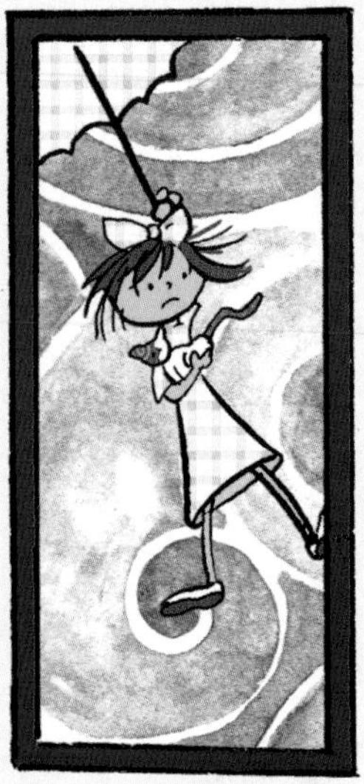

Lucy opened her umbrella and used it to slow their fall, so they drifted down to Earth in just a little less than four days.

They landed back in the square of the very village they had left so long ago, and it seemed as if it had not changed at all.

"You know," Lucy said, "before we left, I wanted nothing more than to live the rest of my life on the moon, but now that we're back, I can't imagine why we ever left."

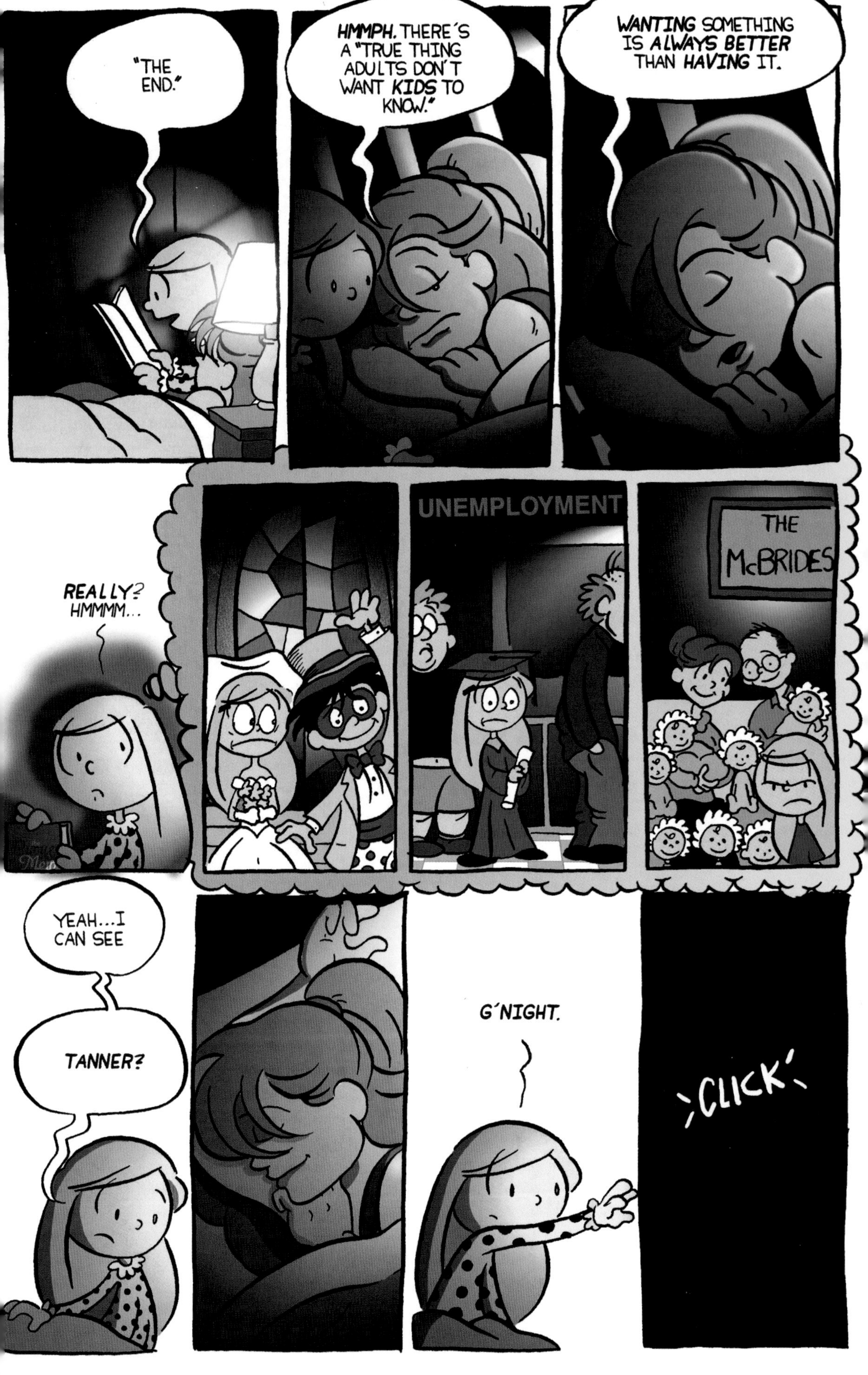
"THE END."
HMMPH. THERE'S A "TRUE THING ADULTS DON'T WANT KIDS TO KNOW."
WANTING SOMETHING IS ALWAYS BETTER THAN HAVING IT.
REALLY? HMMMM...
UNEMPLOYMENT
THE McBRIDES
YEAH...I CAN SEE
TANNER?
G'NIGHT.
CLICK

I COULDN'T STOP THINKING ABOUT THE **SHOW** AND WHY TANNER QUIT SINGING. IT WASN'T LIKE HER TO BE A **QUITTER!** SO THE NEXT DAY AFTER SCHOOL, I DECIDED TO TRY TO WEASEL SOME INFO OUT OF **MOM**.

I WAS **SURPRISED**, CUZ MOM SEEMED KINDA **HAPPY** TO TALK ABOUT IT. SHE TOLD ME THAT WHEN TANNER WAS OUT IN CALIFORNIA AND **LATER** WHEN SHE WAS ON TOUR, THAT THEY DIDN'T REALLY **TALK MUCH**. I GUESS NO ONE THOUGHT TANNER SHOULD BE DOING WHAT SHE WAS DOING, CUZ SHE WAS SO SMART AND ALL.

(**PLUS** NO ONE **LIKED** THAT ERNIE CREEP.)

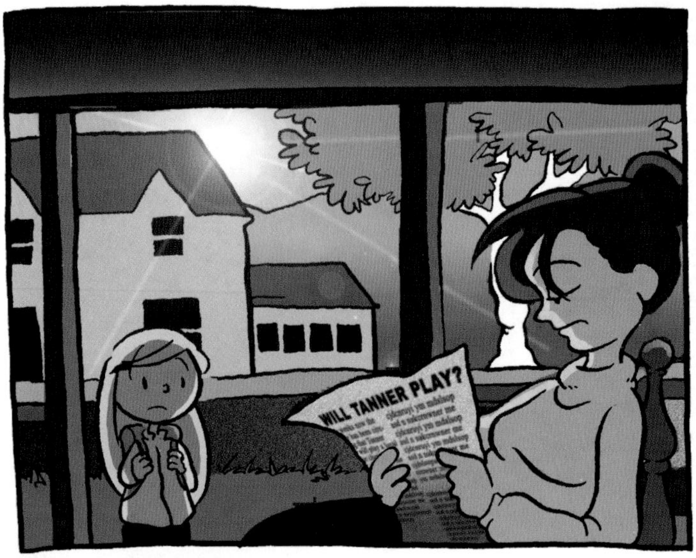
WILL TANNER PLAY?

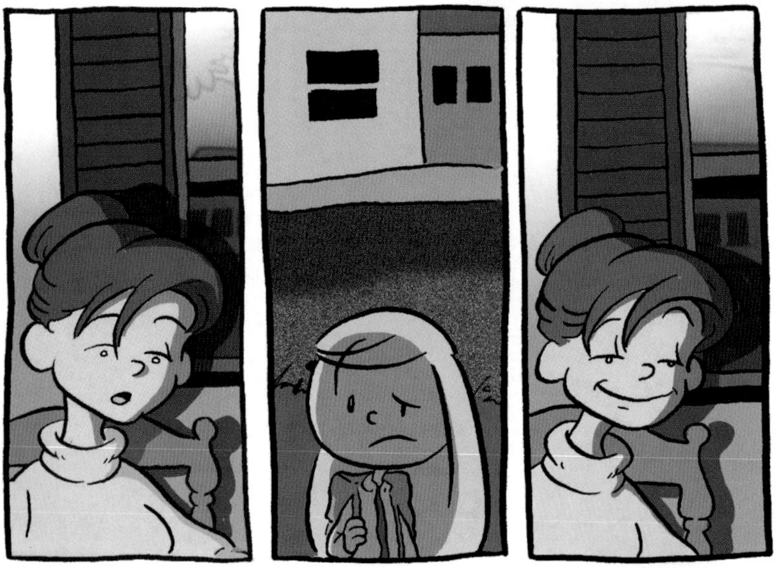

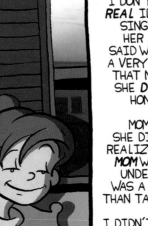

I DON'T THINK MOM HAD ANY **REAL** IDEA WHY TANNER QUIT SINGING. WHEN I **ASKED** HER ABOUT IT, ALL SHE SAID WAS THAT TANNER WAS A VERY **HONEST** PERSON AND THAT NOT ALL THE PEOPLE SHE **DEALT** WITH WERE AS HONEST AS TANNER IS.

MOM ALSO SAID THAT SHE DIDN'T THINK TANNER REALIZED HOW BIG A **FAN** MY **MOM** WAS. SHE SAID **SHE** UNDERSTOOD WHY TANNER WAS A SINGER EVEN BETTER THAN TANNER **HERSELF** DID.

I DIDN'T REALLY UNDERSTAND WHAT SHE **MEANT**, BUT I THINK I DO **NOW**.

THEN MOM LET LOOSE WITH **THIS** BOMBSHELL: SHE HAD KEPT A COLLECTION OF **SOUVENIRS** FROM TANNER'S CAREER. MAGAZINES AND VIDEOS AND TAPES AND STUFF TANNER **HERSELF** PROBABLY DIDN'T EVEN REMEMBER. SHE SAID THAT EVEN THOUGH TANNER DIDN'T WANT TO LOOK AT THAT STUFF **NOW**, SHE WOULD **SOMEDAY**. AND THEN SHE'D REALIZE HOW **BIG A FAN** MY MOM HAD BEEN.

SHE SAID SHE HAD IT ALL IN A TRUNK IN THE **ATTIC**.

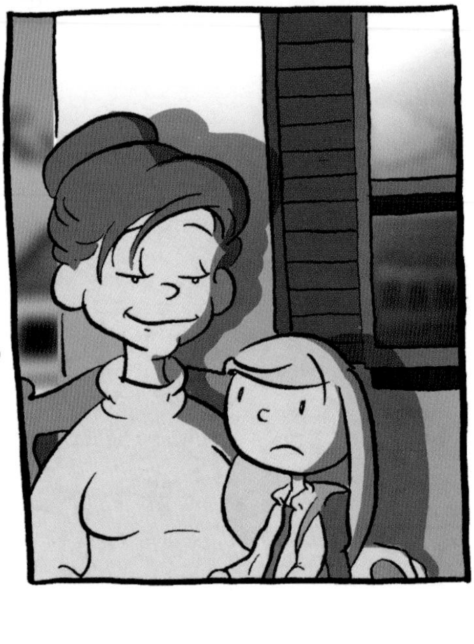

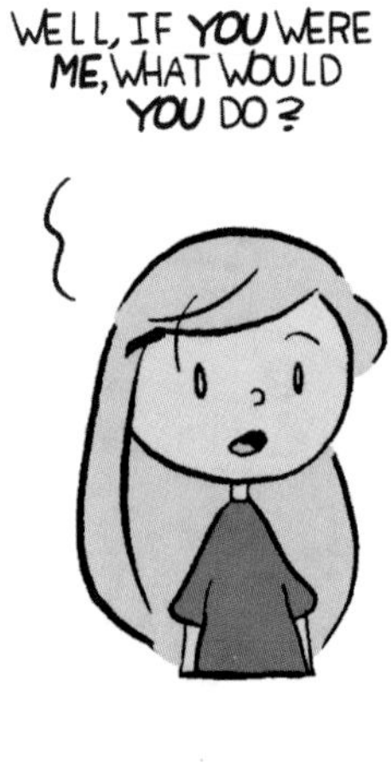
WELL, IF YOU WERE ME, WHAT WOULD YOU DO?

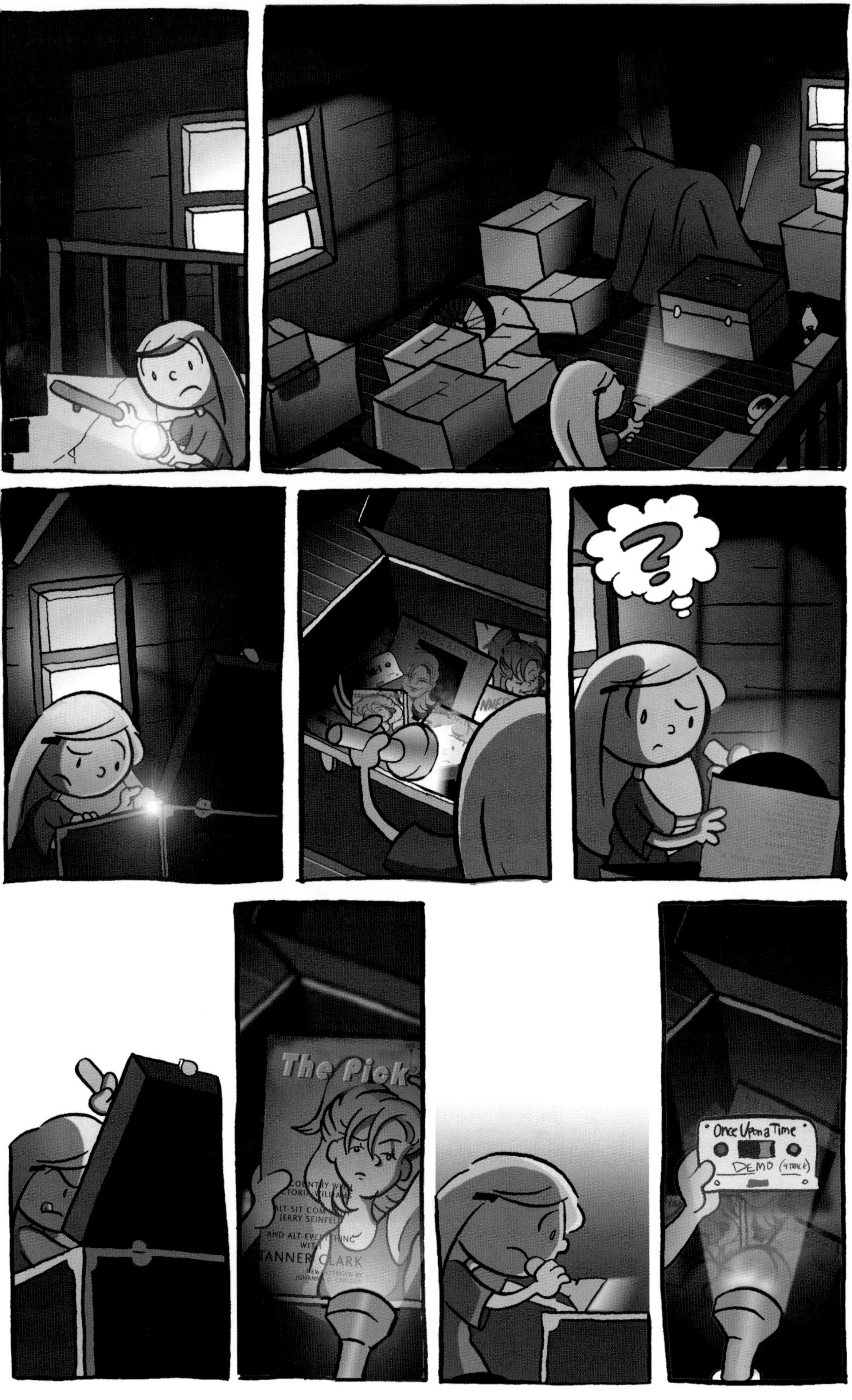
?
The Pick
COUNTRY WITH
CTORIA WILLIAMS
ALT-SIT COM
JERRY SEINFELD
AND ALT-EVERYTHING
WITH
TANNER CLARK
Once Upon a Time
DEMO (4 TRACK)

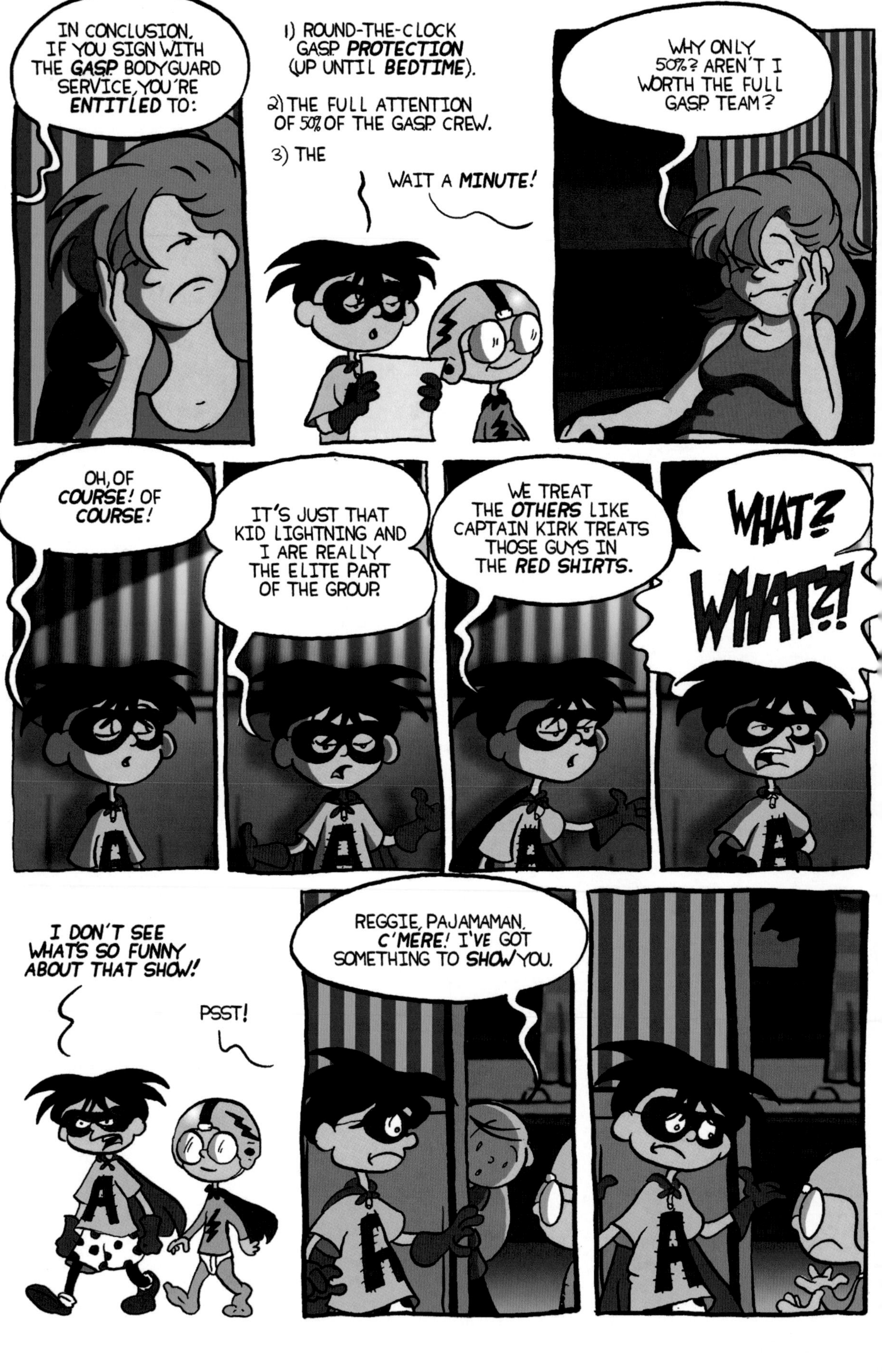
IN CONCLUSION, IF YOU SIGN WITH THE GASP BODYGUARD SERVICE, YOU'RE ENTITLED TO:
1) ROUND-THE-CLOCK GASP PROTECTION (UP UNTIL BEDTIME).
2) THE FULL ATTENTION OF 50% OF THE GASP CREW.
3) THE
WAIT A MINUTE!
WHY ONLY 50%? AREN'T I WORTH THE FULL GASP TEAM?
OH, OF COURSE! OF COURSE!
IT'S JUST THAT KID LIGHTNING AND I ARE REALLY THE ELITE PART OF THE GROUP.
WE TREAT THE OTHERS LIKE CAPTAIN KIRK TREATS THOSE GUYS IN THE RED SHIRTS.
WHAT?
WHAT?!
I DON'T SEE WHAT'S SO FUNNY ABOUT THAT SHOW!
PSST!
REGGIE, PAJAMAMAN, C'MERE! I'VE GOT SOMETHING TO SHOW YOU.

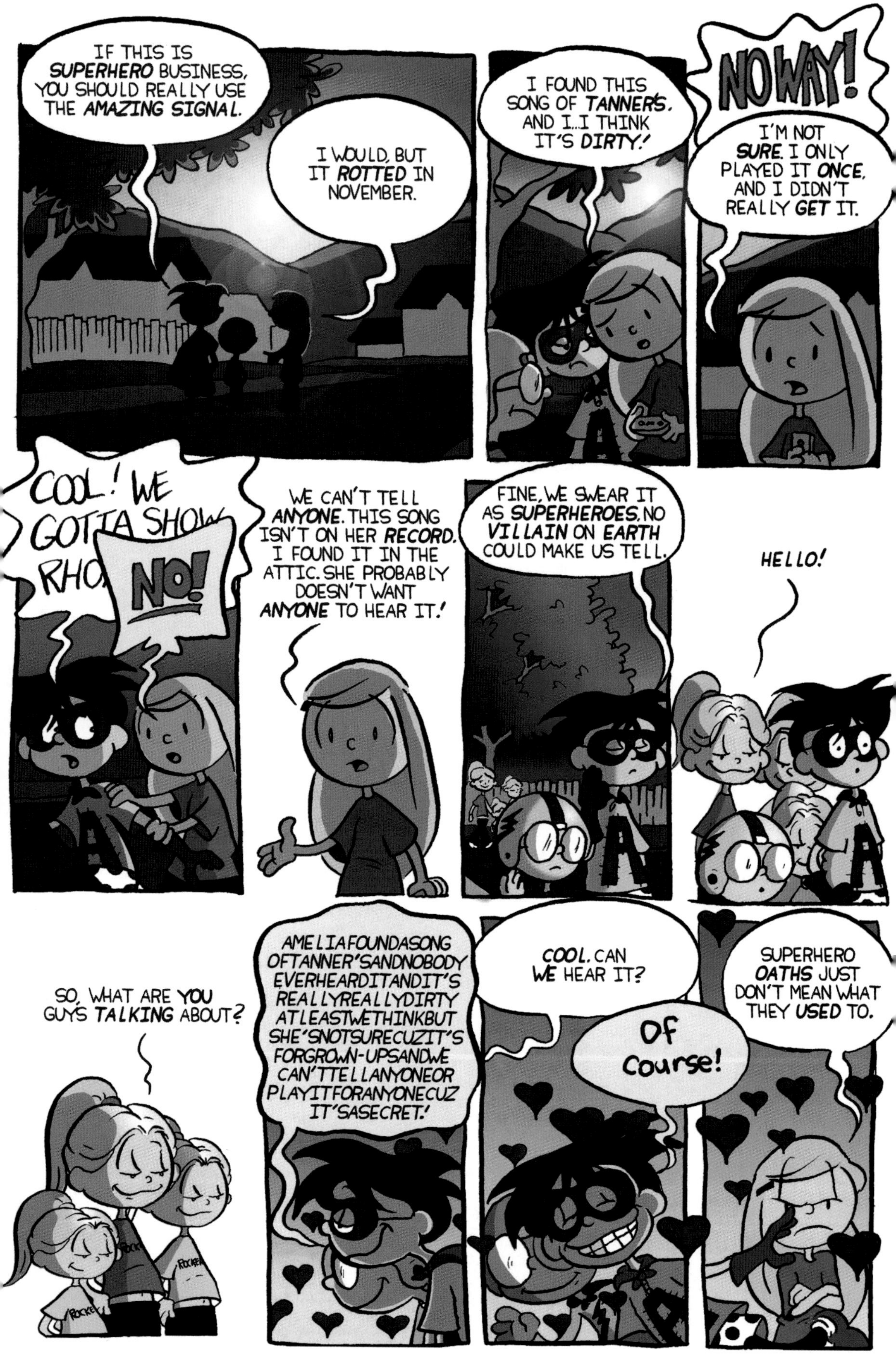

IF THIS IS SUPERHERO BUSINESS, YOU SHOULD REALLY USE THE AMAZING SIGNAL.
I WOULD, BUT IT ROTTED IN NOVEMBER.
I FOUND THIS SONG OF TANNER'S. AND I...I THINK IT'S DIRTY!
NO WAY!
I'M NOT SURE. I ONLY PLAYED IT ONCE, AND I DIDN'T REALLY GET IT.
COOL! WE GOTTA SHOW RHO
NO!
WE CAN'T TELL ANYONE. THIS SONG ISN'T ON HER RECORD. I FOUND IT IN THE ATTIC. SHE PROBABLY DOESN'T WANT ANYONE TO HEAR IT!
FINE, WE SWEAR IT AS SUPERHEROES. NO VILLAIN ON EARTH COULD MAKE US TELL.
HELLO!
SO, WHAT ARE YOU GUYS TALKING ABOUT?
AMELIAFOUNDASONG OFTANNER'SANDNOBODY EVERHEARDITANDIT'S REALLYREALLYDIRTY ATLEASTWETHINKBUT SHE'SNOTSURECUZIT'S FORGROWN-UPSANDWE CAN'TTELLANYONEOR PLAYITFORANYONECUZ IT'SASECRET!
COOL. CAN WE HEAR IT?
Of Course!
SUPERHERO OATHS JUST DON'T MEAN WHAT THEY USED TO.

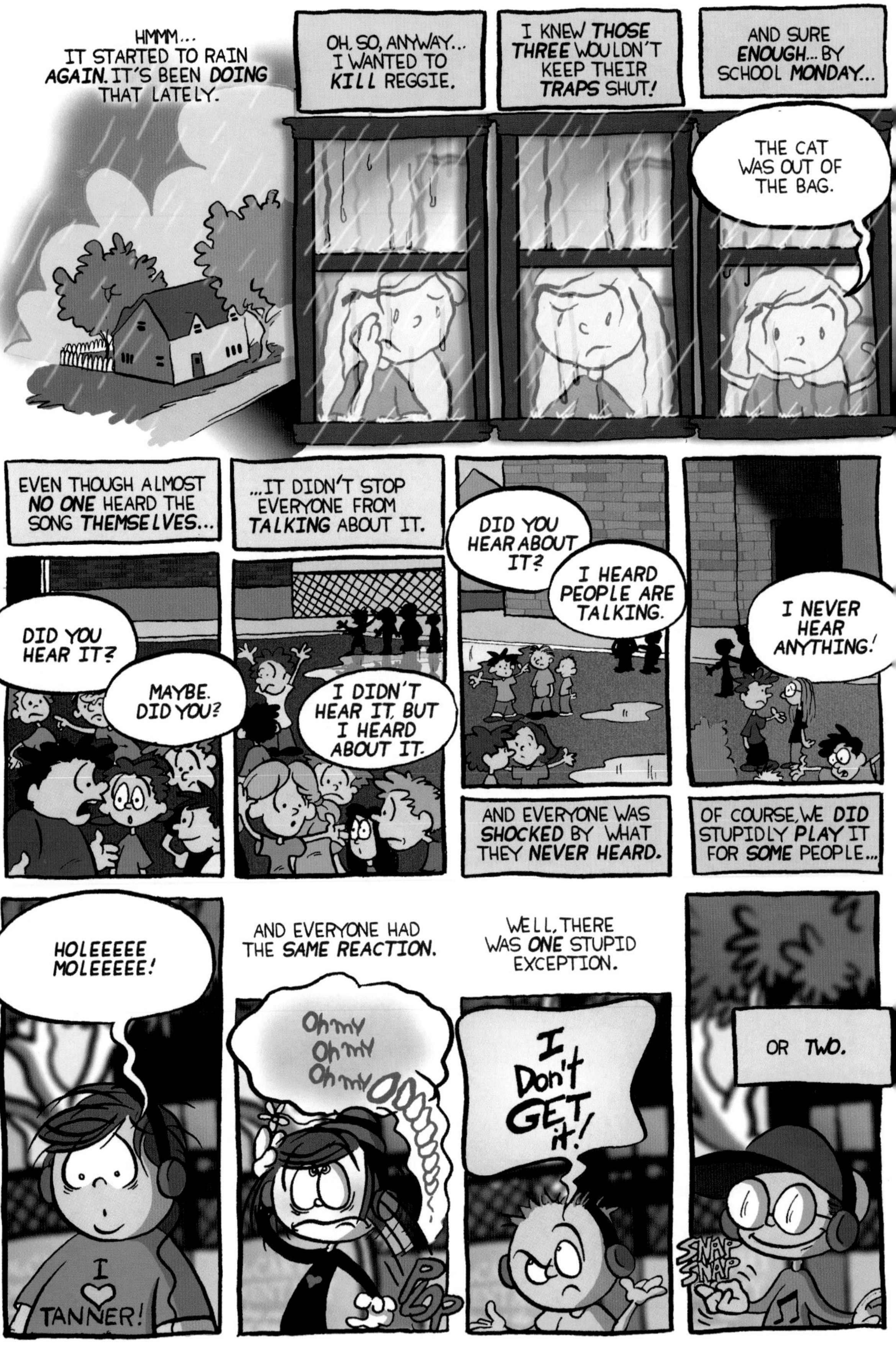
HMMM...
IT STARTED TO RAIN AGAIN. IT'S BEEN DOING THAT LATELY.
OH, SO, ANYWAY... I WANTED TO KILL REGGIE.
I KNEW THOSE THREE WOULDN'T KEEP THEIR TRAPS SHUT!
AND SURE ENOUGH... BY SCHOOL MONDAY...
THE CAT WAS OUT OF THE BAG.
EVEN THOUGH ALMOST NO ONE HEARD THE SONG THEMSELVES...
DID YOU HEAR IT?
MAYBE. DID YOU?
...IT DIDN'T STOP EVERYONE FROM TALKING ABOUT IT.
I DIDN'T HEAR IT, BUT I HEARD ABOUT IT.
DID YOU HEAR ABOUT IT?
I HEARD PEOPLE ARE TALKING.
AND EVERYONE WAS SHOCKED BY WHAT THEY NEVER HEARD.
I NEVER HEAR ANYTHING!
OF COURSE, WE DID STUPIDLY PLAY IT FOR SOME PEOPLE...
HOLEEEEE MOLEEEEE!
I ♥ TANNER!
AND EVERYONE HAD THE SAME REACTION.
Oh my Oh my Oh my OOOOOOOO
POP
WELL, THERE WAS ONE STUPID EXCEPTION.
I Don't GET it!
OR TWO.
SNAP SNAP

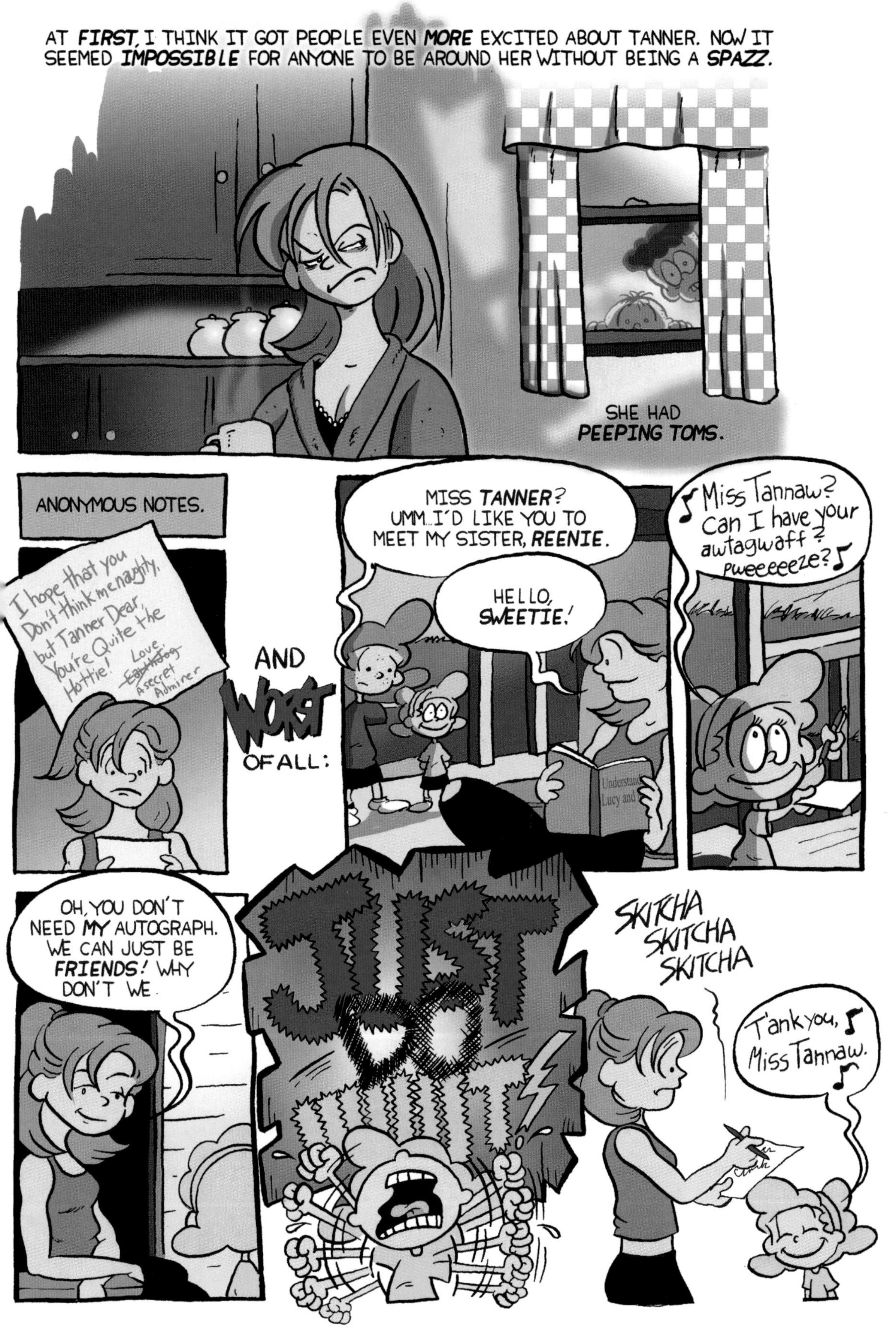
AT FIRST, I THINK IT GOT PEOPLE EVEN MORE EXCITED ABOUT TANNER. NOW IT SEEMED IMPOSSIBLE FOR ANYONE TO BE AROUND HER WITHOUT BEING A SPAZZ.
SHE HAD PEEPING TOMS.
ANONYMOUS NOTES.
I hope that you Don't think me naughty, but Tanner Dear, You're Quite the Hottie! Love, Asecret Admirer
AND WORST OF ALL:
MISS TANNER? UMM...I'D LIKE YOU TO MEET MY SISTER, REENIE.
HELLO, SWEETIE!
Miss Tannaw? Can I have your awtagwaff? Pweeeeeze?
OH, YOU DON'T NEED MY AUTOGRAPH. WE CAN JUST BE FRIENDS! WHY DON'T WE
JUST DO IT!
SKITCHA SKITCHA SKITCHA
T'ank you, Miss Tannaw.

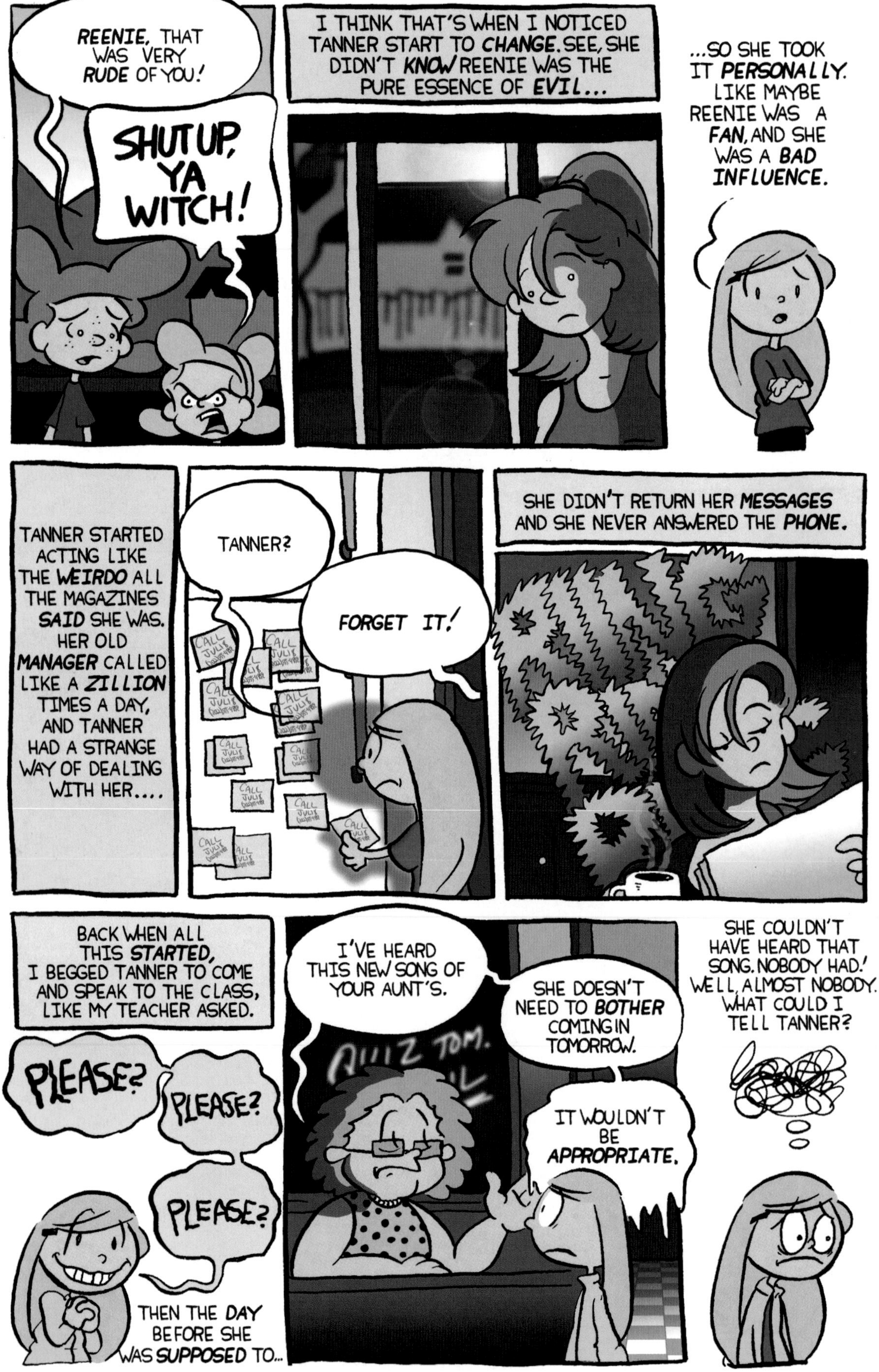
REENIE, THAT WAS VERY RUDE OF YOU!
SHUT UP, YA WITCH!
I THINK THAT'S WHEN I NOTICED TANNER START TO CHANGE. SEE, SHE DIDN'T KNOW REENIE WAS THE PURE ESSENCE OF EVIL...
...SO SHE TOOK IT PERSONALLY. LIKE MAYBE REENIE WAS A FAN, AND SHE WAS A BAD INFLUENCE.
TANNER STARTED ACTING LIKE THE WEIRDO ALL THE MAGAZINES SAID SHE WAS. HER OLD MANAGER CALLED LIKE A ZILLION TIMES A DAY, AND TANNER HAD A STRANGE WAY OF DEALING WITH HER....
TANNER?
FORGET IT!
SHE DIDN'T RETURN HER MESSAGES AND SHE NEVER ANSWERED THE PHONE.
BACK WHEN ALL THIS STARTED, I BEGGED TANNER TO COME AND SPEAK TO THE CLASS, LIKE MY TEACHER ASKED.
PLEASE?
PLEASE?
PLEASE?
THEN THE DAY BEFORE SHE WAS SUPPOSED TO...
I'VE HEARD THIS NEW SONG OF YOUR AUNT'S.
SHE DOESN'T NEED TO BOTHER COMING IN TOMORROW.
IT WOULDN'T BE APPROPRIATE.
SHE COULDN'T HAVE HEARD THAT SONG. NOBODY HAD! WELL, ALMOST NOBODY. WHAT COULD I TELL TANNER?

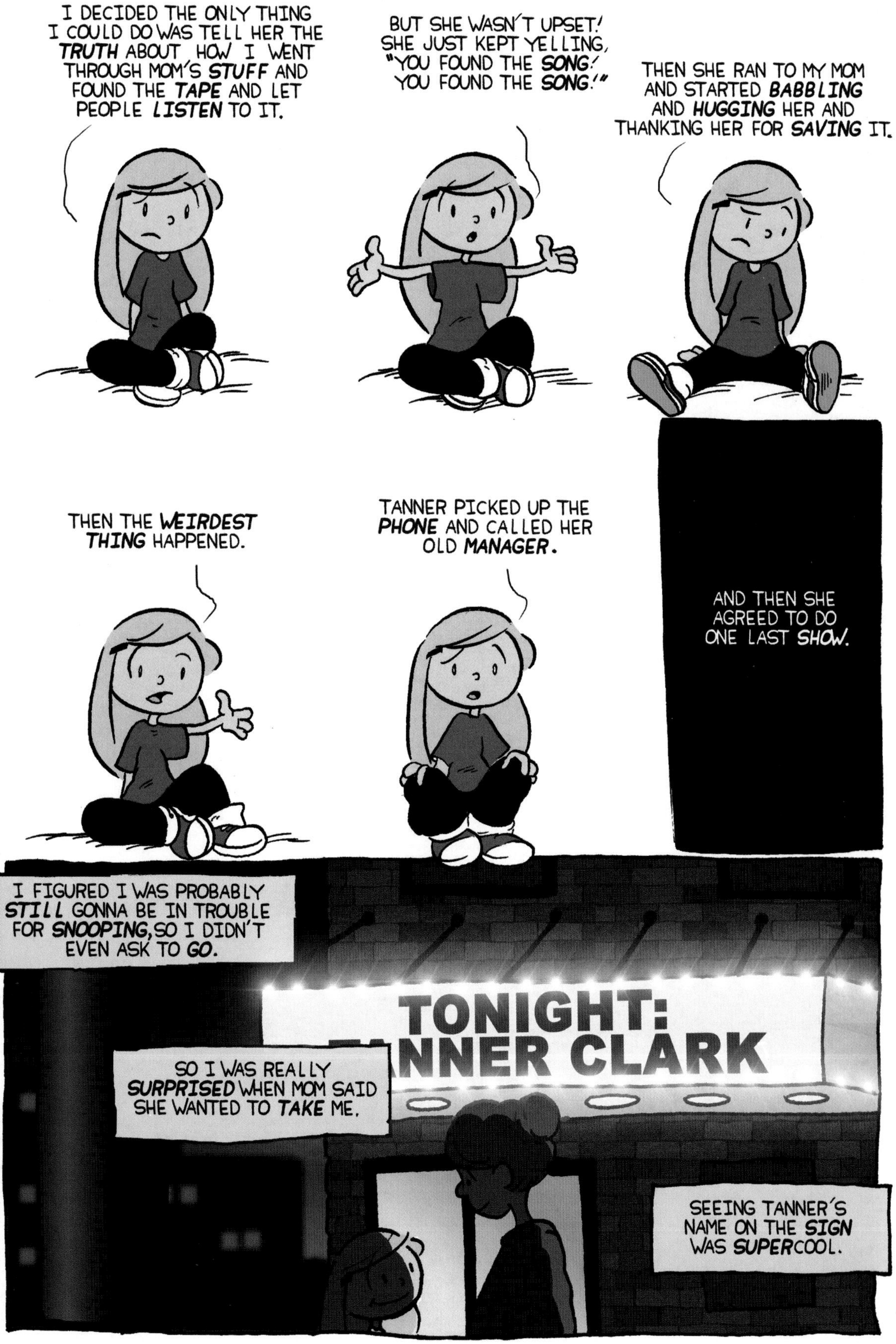
I DECIDED THE ONLY THING I COULD DO WAS TELL HER THE TRUTH ABOUT HOW I WENT THROUGH MOM'S STUFF AND FOUND THE TAPE AND LET PEOPLE LISTEN TO IT.
BUT SHE WASN'T UPSET! SHE JUST KEPT YELLING, "YOU FOUND THE SONG! YOU FOUND THE SONG!"
THEN SHE RAN TO MY MOM AND STARTED BABBLING AND HUGGING HER AND THANKING HER FOR SAVING IT.
THEN THE WEIRDEST THING HAPPENED.
TANNER PICKED UP THE PHONE AND CALLED HER OLD MANAGER.
AND THEN SHE AGREED TO DO ONE LAST SHOW.
I FIGURED I WAS PROBABLY STILL GONNA BE IN TROUBLE FOR SNOOPING, SO I DIDN'T EVEN ASK TO GO.
TONIGHT:
ANNER CLARK
SO I WAS REALLY SURPRISED WHEN MOM SAID SHE WANTED TO TAKE ME.
SEEING TANNER'S NAME ON THE SIGN WAS SUPERCOOL.

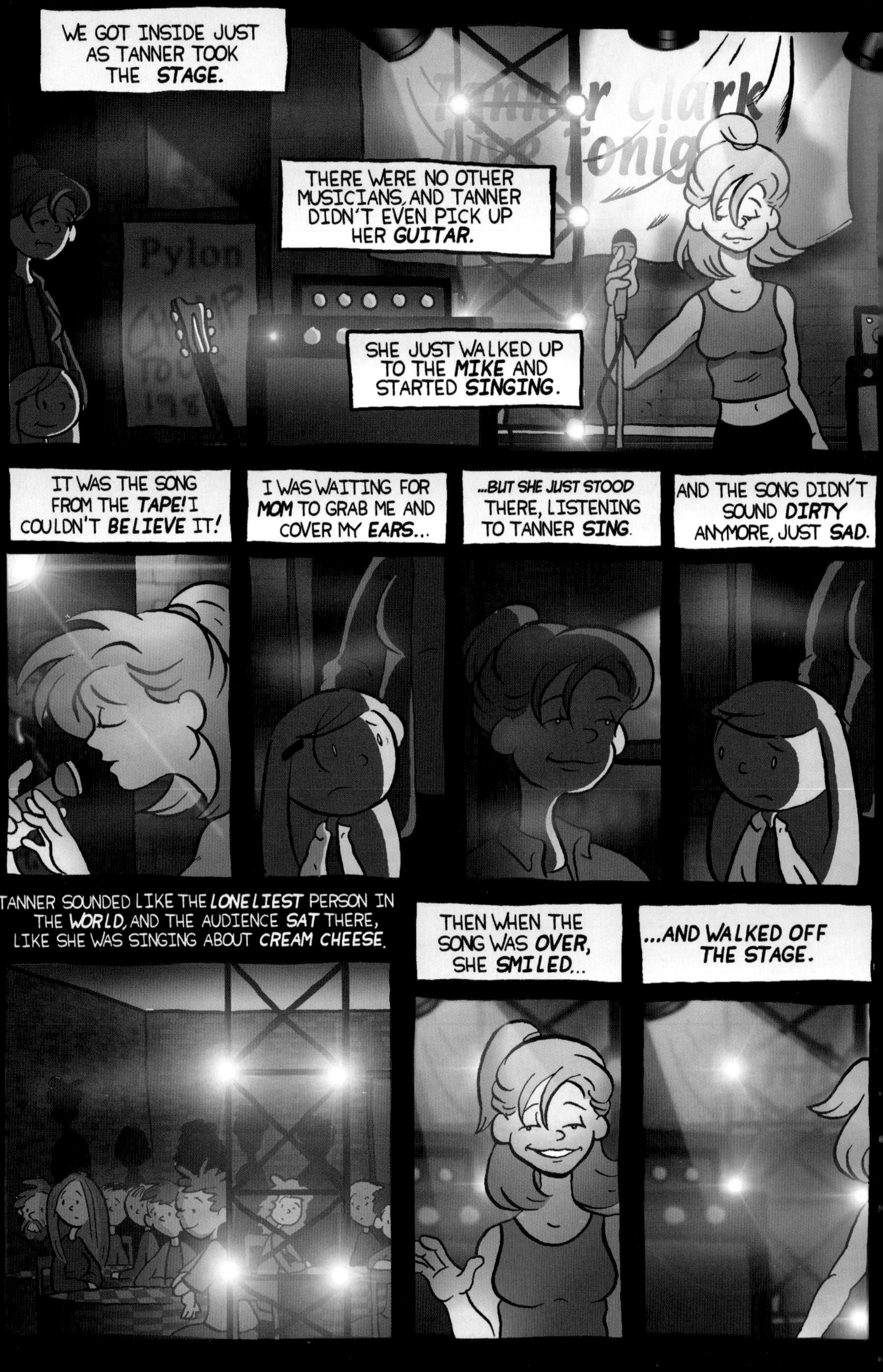
WE GOT INSIDE JUST AS TANNER TOOK THE STAGE.
Tanner Clark Live Tonig
Pylon
THERE WERE NO OTHER MUSICIANS, AND TANNER DIDN'T EVEN PICK UP HER GUITAR.
SHE JUST WALKED UP TO THE MIKE AND STARTED SINGING.
IT WAS THE SONG FROM THE TAPE! I COULDN'T BELIEVE IT!
I WAS WAITING FOR MOM TO GRAB ME AND COVER MY EARS...
...BUT SHE JUST STOOD THERE, LISTENING TO TANNER SING.
AND THE SONG DIDN'T SOUND DIRTY ANYMORE, JUST SAD.
TANNER SOUNDED LIKE THE LONELIEST PERSON IN THE WORLD, AND THE AUDIENCE SAT THERE, LIKE SHE WAS SINGING ABOUT CREAM CHEESE.
THEN WHEN THE SONG WAS OVER, SHE SMILED...
...AND WALKED OFF THE STAGE.

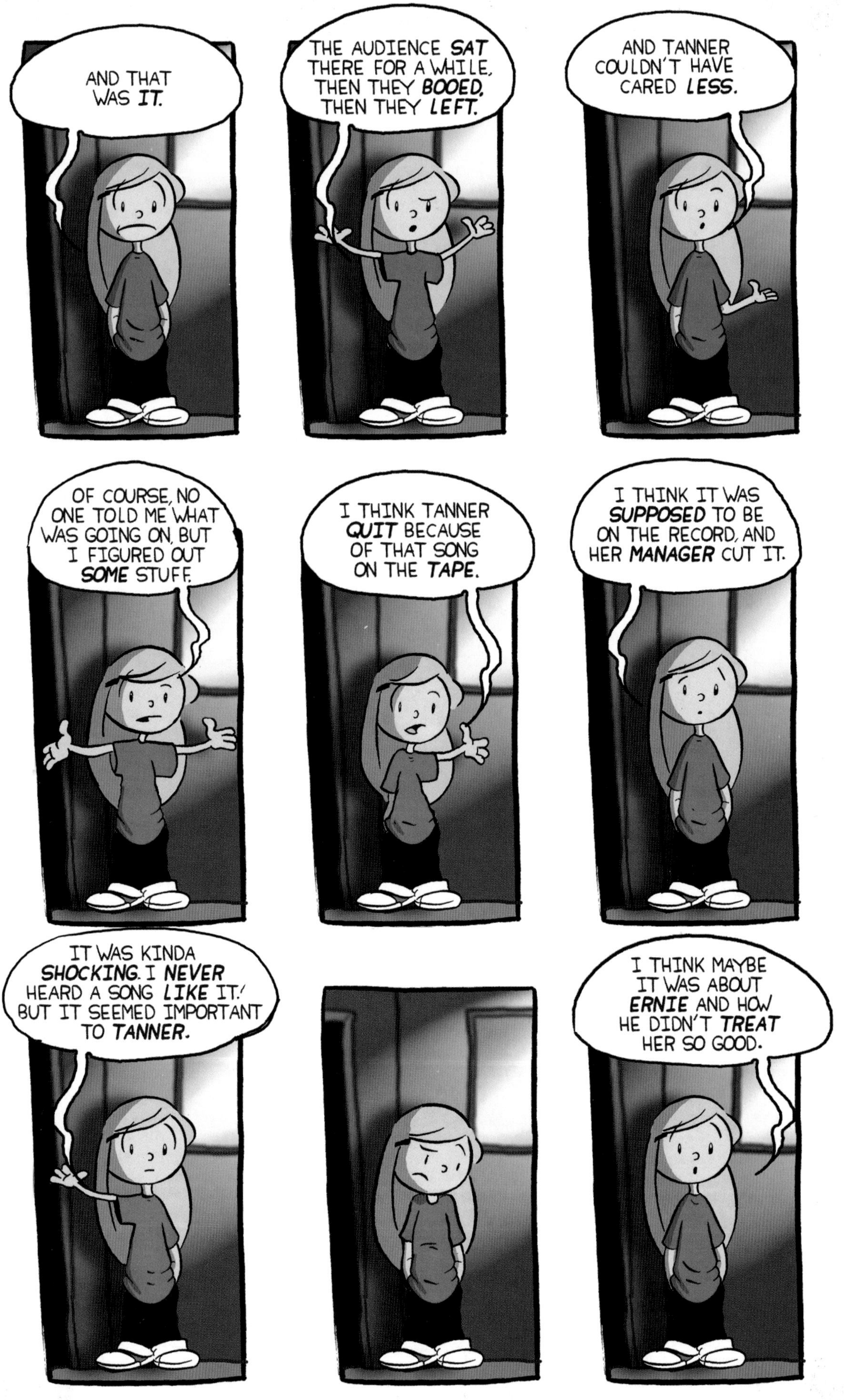
AND THAT WAS IT.
THE AUDIENCE SAT THERE FOR A WHILE, THEN THEY BOOED, THEN THEY LEFT.
AND TANNER COULDN'T HAVE CARED LESS.
OF COURSE, NO ONE TOLD ME WHAT WAS GOING ON, BUT I FIGURED OUT SOME STUFF.
I THINK TANNER QUIT BECAUSE OF THAT SONG ON THE TAPE.
I THINK IT WAS SUPPOSED TO BE ON THE RECORD, AND HER MANAGER CUT IT.
IT WAS KINDA SHOCKING. I NEVER HEARD A SONG LIKE IT! BUT IT SEEMED IMPORTANT TO TANNER.
I THINK MAYBE IT WAS ABOUT ERNIE AND HOW HE DIDN'T TREAT HER SO GOOD.

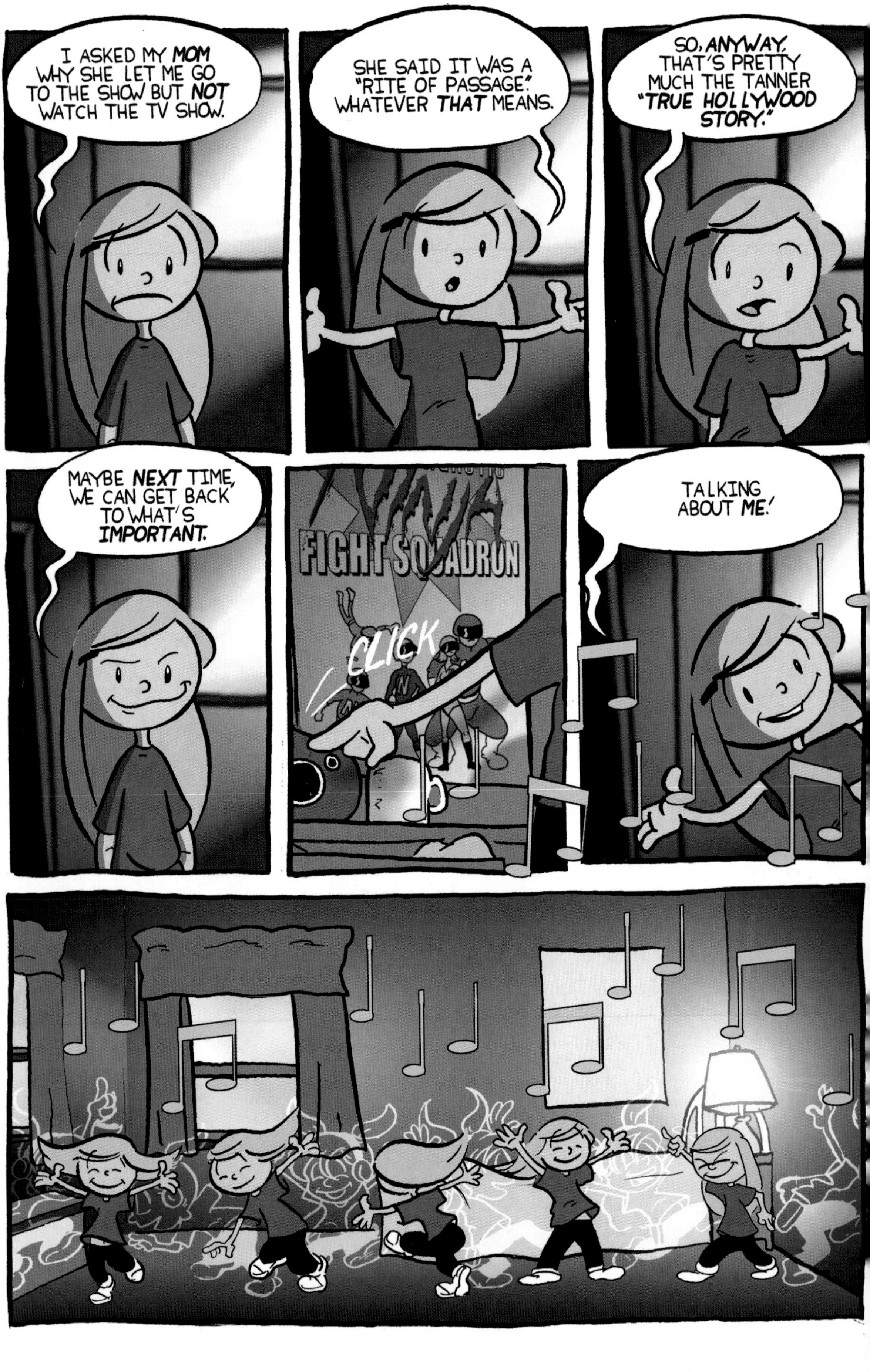
I ASKED MY **MOM** WHY SHE LET ME GO TO THE SHOW BUT **NOT** WATCH THE TV SHOW.
SHE SAID IT WAS A "RITE OF PASSAGE." WHATEVER **THAT** MEANS.
SO, **ANYWAY**, THAT'S PRETTY MUCH THE TANNER **"TRUE HOLLYWOOD STORY."**
MAYBE **NEXT** TIME, WE CAN GET BACK TO WHAT'S **IMPORTANT**.
FIGHT SQUADRON
CLICK
TALKING ABOUT **ME**!